Parnell's boys had had their fun with him, all right. They'd tried to gun him down more times than even a slow-tempered saddle tramp would sit still for.

Now Conagher was too tired and too mean to be played with anymore.

"Parnell," he said, "you've given me grief. All I'm going to give you is a running start . . ."

CONAGHER
Another Thundering Action Novel of the West
by LOUIS L'AMOUR

Bantam Books by Louis L'Amour
Ask your bookseller for the books you have missed

BENDIGO SHAFTER
BORDEN CHANTRY
BRIONNE
THE BROKEN GUN
BUCKSKIN RUN
THE BURNING HILLS
THE CALIFORNIOS
CALLAGHEN
CATLOW
CHANCY
THE CHEROKEE TRAIL
COMSTOCK LODE
CONAGHER
DARK CANYON
DOWN THE LONG HILLS
THE EMPTY LAND
FAIR BLOWS THE WIND
FALLON
THE FERGUSON RIFLE
THE FIRST FAST DRAW
FLINT
GUNS OF THE TIMBER-LAND
HANGING WOMAN CREEK
THE HIGH GRADERS
HIGH LONESOME
HOW THE WEST WAS WON
THE IRON MARSHAL
THE KEY-LOCK MAN
KID RODELO
KILLOE
KILRONE
KIOWA TRAIL
THE MAN CALLED NOON
THE MAN FROM SKIBBEREEN
MATAGORDA
MILO TALON
THE MOUNTAIN VALLEY WAR
NORTH TO THE RAILS
OVER ON THE DRY SIDE
THE PROVING TRAIL
THE QUICK AND THE DEAD

RADIGAN
REILLYS LUCK
THE RIDER OF LOST CREEK
RIVERS WEST
THE SHADOW RIDERS
SHALAKO
SHOWDOWN AT YELLOW BUTTE
SILVER CANYON
SITKA
THE STRONG SHALL LIVE
TAGGART
TUCKER
UNDER THE SWEET-WATER RIM
WAR PARTY
WESTWARD THE TIDE
WHERE THE LONG GRASS BLOWS
YONDERING

Sackett Titles by
Louis L'Amour

1. SACKETT'S LAND
2. TO THE FAR BLUE MOUNTAINS
3. THE DAYBREAKERS
4. SACKETT
5. LANDO
6. MOJAVE CROSSING
7. THE SACKETT BRAND
8. THE LONELY MEN
9. TREASURE MOUNTAIN
10. MUSTANG MAN
11. GALLOWAY
12. THE SKY-LINERS
13. THE MAN FROM THE BROKEN HILLS
14. RIDE THE DARK TRAIL
15. THE WARRIOR'S PATH
16. LONELY ON THE MOUNTAIN

Louis L'Amour
Conagher

W
L'Amour
1982

BANTAM BOOKS
TORONTO • NEW YORK • LONDON • SYDNEY • AUCKLAND

CONAGHER

A Bantam Book / September 1969
2nd printing . . . . March 1970
3rd printing . . . . June 1970
4th printing . . . . . . August 1971
New Bantam edition / June 1971

2nd printing .. October 1971	12th printing .... February 1977
3rd printing . February 1972	13th printing . . . . July 1977
4th printing ... August 1972	14th printing ... November 1977
5th printing .. January 1973	15th printing ... December 1977
6th printing . September 1973	16th printing ... December 1978
7th printing . November 1973	17th printing ... September 1979
8th printing ... August 1974	18th printing . . . . May 1980
9th printing .. October 1975	19th printing ... September 1981
10th printing .. February 1976	20th printing . . . . July 1982
11th printing . . . . . May 1976	21st printing ... December 1982

Photograph of Louis L'Amour by
John Hamilton—Globe Photos, Inc.

ISBN: 0-553-22843-9

Published simultaneously in the United States and Canada

Bantam Books are published by Bantam Books, Inc. Its trade-
mark, consisting of the words "Bantam Books" and the por-
trayal of a rooster, is registered in the United States Patent
Office and in other countries. Marca Registrada. Bantam
Books, Inc., 666 Fifth Avenue, New York, New York 10103.

PRINTED IN THE UNITED STATES OF AMERICA

H   30 29 28 27 26 25

To Richard L. Waldo

The land lay empty around them, lonely and still. On their right a ridge of hills with scattered cedars, on their left an open plain sweeping to a far horizon that offered a purple hint of hills. In all that vastness there was nothing but the creak and groan of the wagon, and overhead the sky, brassy with sunlight.

"It's only a couple of miles now," Jacob told her. "Just around that point of rocks." He pointed with his whipstock.

She felt her heart shriveling within her. "It's awfully dry, isn't it?"

"It's dry," Jacob's tone was abrupt. "It's been a bad year."

The team plodded, heads bobbing with weariness. The last town was fifty miles behind them, the last ranch almost as far. In all that distance they had seen not a ranch, a claim shack, or a fence . . . not a horse, a cow, or even a track.

At last he said, "I did not promise you much, and it is not much, but the land is ours, and what the land becomes will be ours, too. The land is not only what it is, it is what we make it."

The heavy wagon rumbled on, endlessly, monotonously. The heat was stifling, their pace so slow they could not escape the dust. It settled over their clothing, their eyebrows, in the folds of their skin. The children, weary with the heat, had fallen asleep, and for that she was thankful.

The wagon reached the point of rocks, bumped over a flat rock, then rounded the point.

Her heart sank. Before them, and close under the shoulder of a hill, was a cabin, a solitary building, square and bare, without shed or corral, without shrubs, without a tree.

"There it is!" There was pride in Jacob's tone. "There's our house, Evie."

She knew how he felt, for in the three years of their life together she had learned this about him: that he had never known a home, had never possessed anything of his own beyond the clothes he wore, and his tools. He had worked hard to save the money for this move.

Drab it might be, barren it was, but to Jacob, a middle-aged man with years of hard work behind him, it was home. She warned herself that she must never forget that, and that she must do what she could to help him.

"We will plant trees, we will drill a well . . . you wait and see. First, I must buy some stock. We must have cattle."

The wagon rolled down a slight grade, and at long last they drew up at the door. The cabin was small, but it was well-built. The cloud of dust settled down over them, settled at last.

Laban awoke and sat up groggily. "Pa, are we there? Are we home?" he asked.

"Get down, son. We are here."

Jacob walked to the door, fiddled with it a moment, then swung it wide. "Come, Evie, we have much to do. I must ride out when morning comes. There is no time to waste."

Evie hesitated, hoping that this once he might help her down. He need not carry her across the threshold . . . after all, she was no new bride.

Still, it was their first home, and he had forgotten her, his mind already busy with the problems of the place. He was letting down the tail gate, while Laban and Ruth ran to the door to peek inside.

"Pa!" Ruth called. "There's no floor! It's just dirt!"

"It will have to do," he said testily.

Evie got down and removed her hat, fluffed a little dust from her hair and went into the cabin. She knew just what to do, and knew what had to come into the house first. Hers was an orderly mind when it came to such things, and she had planned for this when they packed the wagon.

There was little to move. Before nightfall a meal was on the table, beds were made, a breakfast fire was laid, and the little world that revolved around Evie was once more established and ready for the morrow.

The cabin was built of native stone taken from the ridge back of the house, and it consisted of one large room. It had a peaked roof, with a loft and a ladder that reached to it. There was a large fireplace, a square table, a double bed, two chairs and a bench. The floor was of hard-packed earth. The water had to be carried from a water hole about twenty-five yards back of the house, and about twenty feet higher up the slope.

The children would sit on the bench at meals, and they would sleep in the loft, on pallets. The loft would be, as she well knew, the warmest part of the cabin.

"The first cattle we sell," Jacob said, "we will put in a board floor."

The first cattle they sold . . . would that be two years away? Or maybe three?

Three years on a dirt floor? She had always been poor, but not that poor. But she said nothing, for she had never complained; she never would complain. Jacob had thought of this too long, and he would need help, not complaints or arguments.

They were here, and he still had four hundred dollars with which to buy cattle. He had dreamed of this, as he had told her, long before they were married—even before he had married the first time, before the children were born. . . . One hundred and sixty acres and a cabin built with his own hands.

He had built well, for that was his trade. He was a steady, hard-working man, skilled at both the carpenter's and the mason's trade, but he had managed to save little during the hard years of depression and struggle, during his first wife's long illness, and the constant loans to his brother-in-law, Tom Evers.

That, at least, was one thing they had left behind. Tom Evers had been gone on one of his forays when they left Ohio, and was safely behind them.

At daybreak, after a quick breakfast, Jacob stood with her a few minutes, looking toward the east. "I shall be gone several weeks. You have supplies enough, and you will have no need for money, but I have put aside fifty dollars that I do not need for cattle. Use it only if there is need."

It was not much, but it was the first money she had held in her hands since her father had died and left her two hundred dollars. When only five dollars was left of that money she had married Jacob Teale, a widower with two children. He was a stern but kind man, but bad luck had dogged him as if it owned him, and after three years they had this . . . no more.

"You will have the shotgun," he said, "and Laban is a good hunter. There are quail here, and sage hens. He might get a close-up shot at a deer. And you have supplies for at least a month, if you are careful."

They stood in the doorway, Evie and the children, and watched him ride away on the sorrel, a straight, stiff-backed man, filled with plans and determination, who gave no thought to the imponderables, the little things upon which fortunes are made or broken.

Evie went back into the cabin and sat down at the table.

Her father had been a dreamer and a drifter, filled with excellent advice which he never applied to himself. "Evie," he would say, "when in doubt, sit down and think. It is only the mind of man that has lifted him above the animals."

She must consider now. This was a time of drouth. The heat had parched and baked the land, sucking away the moisture from the grass, leaving the trees like tinder.

Jacob would be gone for weeks. There must be something to show when he returned, some things accomplished of which she could say, "There . . . this I have done."

But there was something else to consider. For there was the sky, and there was the vast and lonely land, and there was little in either on which the mind could feed, not her eager mind, restless, probing, seeking.

She must be busy, and the children must be busy. There were the three horses to be cared for. They must be fed, watered, ridden occasionally or worked. Laban was eleven, but he had worked beside his father, and for neighbors. He had milked cows, chopped wood, helped with the harvest. He was a strong, honest boy, and she thought he liked her.

Ruth was quick, imaginative, outgoing. She, perhaps more than any of them, needed people.

So she formed her plans.

They must explore the country around. They must spade up a kitchen garden and ditch it for irrigation from the spring. They must find what grass there was, and wood must be cut for the fires now and those of the winter to come. There would be much hard work, but there must be other things, too. There must be amusement . . . something to do after work, and above all she must remember that Laban must be given more freedom, more responsibility, without forgetting that he was still a boy, a very young boy.

The land that lay before them was so empty. It was brown where it was not gray. Once this land had been a lake bed, but that was long ago, in some vanished time. Now there was before them just dry grass stretching away into the distance. Back of them lay the brown, cedar-clad hills.

"Laban," she said, "we must explore. We will need more water for the stock, and there may be another water hole. We shall look for it."

He looked at her. "Yes, ma'am, but . . . but maybe there's Indians."

Her eyes searched his face. "What makes you say that?"

"I heard them talking at Socorro. There's 'Paches in the mountains, and sometimes there's others, wild ones who come up from the border."

She did not know whether to believe him or not. Jacob had said nothing about Indians, and she had heard no such talk. But Laban was a straightforward, trustworthy boy. If he said he had heard such talk, he had heard it . . . or what he thought was that.

They made a slow half-circle through the hills behind the cabin. There was a good deal of wood lying around among the cedars, deadfalls, or lightning-struck or fallen limbs. For a season at least they would have no worries about fuel. She also saw several good-sized logs lying about. "If we could only get them up to the cabin," she said.

"We could snake 'em up," Laban said. "Hitch to

'em with a chain or a rope and haul them right up. We could use ol' Black. He's steady."

By sundown Jacob Teale was twenty miles east and turning up a draw to find a place to camp for the night. A small arroyo lay just over the crest, he recalled, and beyond it was a thick clump of cedar. There was a hollow there among the rocks where water often collected. He turned up the bank of the draw, rode over the ridge and into the arroyo. His horse slid down the steep bank, and started up the opposite side.

A hoof came down on a loose slab of rock which gave way, and the horse fell, struggling for a foothold, then rolled over. Jacob's boot caught in the stirrup and when the horse rolled the pommel came down hard on his chest.

Something snapped inside. He felt no pain, no shock, only a kind of surprise.

Death, he had imagined, was dramatic, and filled with pain; or one died in bed with friends around, slowly, of an illness. The horse struggled, lunged, tried to rise, and fell back. And this time there was pain . . . a crushing, terrible, strangling pain.

But he was free of the horse's weight, even though his foot was still trapped beneath it. Somehow he rolled to an elbow and looked down at himself. His shirt and coat were red with blood. He felt faint and sick. Then he looked at the horse.

One leg was broken, an ugly compound fracture with the naked bone exposed.

He felt for his gun, drew it slowly and carefully. "Sorry, Ben," he said, and shot the horse in the head.

It stiffened sharply, then lay still.

A moment longer he remained on his elbow. He looked at the evening sky, where a star had appeared; he looked at the dusty arroyo, the bloody saddle. He could not live; even had there been a doctor, he knew that nothing could be done for him. The gun stayed in his hand, but it was not in him to use it.

He lay back, feeling a tearing within his chest. He looked up at the sky and said, "Evie . . . Evie, what have I done to you? . . . Laban . . . Ruthie . . . Lab . . ."

He tried to get up then. If he could drag himself back into the trail. If he could get back where somebody could find him. If he could . . .

He died then, and lay still, and the light wind of evening worried his hair, sifted a little dust into the creases of his clothing.

He died alone, as men in the West so often died, died trying to accomplish something, to build something, to go somewhere. Sometimes the sand buried those men's bodies, sometimes the coyotes scattered their bones, leaving a few buttons, a sun-dried boot heel, a rusted pistol.

Some of them were found and buried, but some dried up and turned to dust and the wind took the dust away. One of these was Jacob Teale.

2

When Jacob Teale had been gone three weeks the stage came by the Teale cabin.

Ruthie saw it first. She was up on the slope gathering chips for kindling when she saw the dust far away up the valley.

For a moment she stared, then, dropping the chips, she ran for the house, calling out, "Ma! Ma! Somebody's coming!"

Evie put down her dishcloth and, drying her hands on her apron, she went to the door. Laban came running from the corral, where he was in the process of building a crude shelter of brush for the three horses and the milk cow they had brought from Missouri, led behind the wagon.

Shading their eyes, they saw the stage coming, galloping horses obscured by the accompanying cloud of dust, and then suddenly the racing teams swung from the trail and came up the road into the yard.

It was a Concord stage drawn by four horses, and two men rode the box. Inside, they could see two other men. The driver pulled up and stared down at them.

"Now where in the Lord's name did you come from?" he demanded.

"I am Mrs. Jacob Teale," Evie replied, with dignity, "and these are my children. Won't you step down? You must be very hungry."

"That we are," the driver agreed. "Ma'am, this here gent is Beaver Sampson. He's riding shotgun. He's riding against Injuns more than road agents.

"The tall gentleman stepping down is Tom Wildy. He's superintendent of this stretch of stage line, God help him, and you will recognize the uniform of the U.S. Cavalry on the other feller. He's Cap'n Hurley. I'm Charlie McCloud, and we're runnin' the first stage through to the Plaza."

"Come in, won't you?" Evie said. "We weren't expecting company, but I am sure we can find something. Laban, will you bring in an armful of wood? I'll make fresh coffee."

Tom Wildy glanced at the stone cabin, then at the corrals. "You will forgive our astonishment, Mrs. Teale.

We were told there was no one in this area at all. Coming upon your place is quite a surprise."

Sampson glanced from her to the children. "Anybody tell you this was Injun country, ma'am?"

"We haven't seen any. Of course, we have stayed close to home. Just gone for wood, and all. Mr. Teale is away at the moment—he has gone to the settlements to buy cattle."

"Teale? I haven't heard the name. Not that I know all the folks who come through, but a man buying cattle . . . well, usually you hear about such things."

Evie led the way into the cabin. "We are not set up for company yet, gentlemen, but you're welcome."

"Thank you," Wildy said, seating himself and holding his hat on his knee. "Mrs. Teale, we'll be running a somewhat makeshift affair for a while, so I wonder if you could take on the feeding of passengers until we get our stations established? Your place here is just twenty miles from our last planned stop, and you could make yourself as well as the company a bit of money. That's scarce, I presume."

"Indeed it is, Mr. Wildy." She smoothed her apron self-consciously. "Yes, I could do that, but we would have to lay in supplies."

"No problem. Mrs. Teale, you would be saving us a lot of trouble and expense if you could handle this until we get settled down. You make up a list of whatever you need and I'll have McCloud bring it on the next stage . . . at our expense. The company will foot the bill to get you started, in consideration of the favor you would be doing us. After that you will have to manage on your own profits."

"That would be fine."

"We will be having another stage stop fifteen miles west, but you could save us the expense of building for the time being."

He turned to Laban. "How are you with horses, son? Could you harness the teams and get them out for us until your pa gets home?"

"Yes, sir. I help pa with the horses, sir. I hitched up and drove when we came west from Missouri."

"You're from Missouri, then?" Captain Hurley said.

"My husband is a Missourian, Captain. I am from Ohio."

As she talked she was moving about, getting things ready. She was flushed and excited. It was a pleasure to have visitors, and she enjoyed hearing them speak of the common places of travel, of road conditions, the possibilities of rain, and the grazing of stock.

"You will be having neighbors to the south," Hurley said. "Some big cattle outfits are moving in about thirty miles down the country."

"It will be a pleasure. Will the stages come often, Mr. Wildy?"

"Not at first. Then they will come every other day. Two, sometimes three a week—one going west, and another going east. It will depend on the business."

She bustled about, getting food on the table and refilling their cups.

Later, when they had eaten and were filing out to get aboard the stage, McCloud lingered. "Ma'am, you keep a sharp watch out for Injuns. They ain't been troublesome right now, but it can start any time, and there's always young bucks out for mischief.

"Don't give 'em anything. If you do, they'll figure it's a sign of fear. Make 'em trade. Any Injun understands trade and they cotton to it, but they're notional, and their thinkin' ain't like ours."

"Thank you, Mr. McCloud. I will remember."

"You say your man went to buy cattle?"

"He was looking for breeding stock. We hope to raise a good herd and start selling in about three years."

"If I see him, I'll tell him you're all well." McCloud touched the brim of his hat. "Be seein' you, ma'am."

They stood out in front of the cabin and watched the stage until it disappeared around the next curve of the road. Then Evie turned. "Come, children," she said. "We've got a lot to do."

All of them felt a new excitement. Laban was puffed up with importance over his new job. He was to be a hostler, at least until pa got home, and even after that if he could talk pa into letting him keep on with it— under pa's supervision, of course.

At sunset Evie walked away from the cabin and stood alone, her hair stirring a little in the faint breeze. She stood on the edge of the trail, a hundred yards from the cabin. All was very still.

She never tired of the mornings and evenings here, the soft lights, the changing colors of sunlight and cloud upon the hills, the stirring of wind in the grass. Out here there was no escaping the sky or the plains, and Evie knew that until she came west she had never really known distance.

The air was incredibly clear. Fresh and cool as it was, one breathed it in like drinking cool water; and always there was a definite odor on it, the odor depending on the direction from which the wind blew: the smell of cedar, and of pines beyond, the smell of sage, or, from the dryer lands after a rain, the smell of the creosote bush.

She looked down now at the tracks in the road, the tracks of the passing stage, the first tracks in their road since Jacob left.

Suddenly, she felt a chill. Superimposed on the tracks of the stage were the tracks of unshod ponies . . . Indian ponies!

When could they have passed? How could she have missed seeing them?

It must have been at suppertime, when they were at the table. The stage had left shortly after noon, and they had worked around the place, inside and out. Laban had fed the stock . . . yes, it must have been at suppertime.

She walked a little way, studying the tracks. There seemed to have been two horses, and at one point the riders had drawn up, facing toward the cabin, perhaps listening to them talking.

That was not over an hour ago. She turned abruptly and, gathering her skirt, started for the cabin. Even now they might be up in the cedars, watching her. She moved quickly.

Laban met her at the door, brushing hay from his clothes. Ruthie was reading a newspaper one of the men had left with them.

"What is it, ma? What's wrong?" Laban asked.

She hesitated for a moment, but they must be told. "Indians, Laban. I saw their tracks in the road. They must have come along while we were eating supper. We must be very careful."

That night she left a crack of the window open looking toward the corrals, and she placed the shotgun beside her. If the Indians came she supposed it would be for the horses, but although the coyotes howled the long night through, she heard no other sound.

Before it was time for the stage to come again, she carefully tamped down the earthen floor, and then, as she had seen her grandmother do years ago on their farm in Ohio, she traced a floral pattern on the floor to resemble a carpet. She was pleased with the result.

When they were expecting the stage she put water on the fire and got food ready to serve, and then they waited.

They heard the stage coming long before it arrived, heard the rattle of the wheels over stones, and the running horses.

Charlie McCloud was driving again, and a different man was riding shotgun. He was a lean, round-shouldered man with a tough face and a hard-cut mouth. He was sporting a cut on his cheekbone and a black eye.

"This here is Kiowa Staples," Charlie said. "It looks like he run into something in the dark."

Staples threw him a hard glance. "It was some no-account saddle bum," Staples said irritably. "I misjudged him. The next time we meet it won't be fists we'll use."

"Aw, forget it Kiowa," Charlie said. "You brought it on yourself. There's some men you just can't push, an' you pushed that one too far. You think it over an' you won't blame him none."

"I won't blame him," Staples replied, "but I'll kill him."

There was one passenger, a portly man in a black derby and black suit who descended stiffly from the stage, stretched, and started toward the house.

"My advice to you, Kiowa, is to leave that gent alone," Charlie McCloud advised. "I've seen his kind before. You don't find them swaggering around hunting trouble, because they've seen trouble a-plenty. They've been up the creek an' over the mountain, they've hunted buffalo an' they've fit Injuns an' maybe outlaws, an' they've done it like you an' me hitch a team of hosses— it's ever'day work to them. You steer clear of that kind if you want to keep a whole hide . . . an' a reputation."

Together McCloud and Kiowa packed the supplies in and placed them on the floor out of the way, while Evie put the food on the table. It was good solid food and all three men ate with relish.

"Stays with you, that kind of grub," Charlie said.

"If I wasn't married, Mrs. Teale, I'd surely come a-courtin'.' "

Evie blushed. "Thank you, Mr. McCloud. I've always liked to see a man enjoy his food."

Kiowa looked up at her. "No Injuns?"

"We saw tracks," Laban said, "right after you folks left, the last time. There were two of them."

"They were scoutin' you," Kiowa said, "and us. You keep a fresh eye, ma'am, and you worry some. It'll likely be your saving."

When they were gone, Evie and Ruthie put the supplies away, while Laban went back to work on the shelter for the animals. It was crudely built and scarcely more than a windbreak, but Evie, watching him from a distance, saw that the boy worked with some assurance and not a little skill. Evidently he had watched his father and others, and perhaps had helped at such jobs before.

Since his father had been gone Laban had been getting up earlier and working harder, and he had fussed much less with Ruthie than before. His sister was mystified by the change. Laban seemed suddenly grown up and far away from her. He went about his work with great seriousness, and did not wait to be asked. He did what needed doing, and Ruthie's respect grew despite herself. She found herself speaking to him as she might to someone much older. At times it irked her, but Laban seemed not to notice; sometimes she deliberately teased him, hoping to arouse his irritation, to make him want to fight back, but he assumed a lofty attitude and only smiled or, worse yet, ignored her.

In the week that passed the stage stopped only twice, and then on the day it was due to come again, three riders appeared, driving a herd of horses, a dozen of them to be left at the Teale place.

One of the cowhands was a youngster, not over

seventeen, the others were older men. Johnny McGivern came galloping on ahead, yelling at Laban. "Open the bars there, boy! We're a-bringin' in the hosses!"

Laban ran to open the gate and the horses streamed in, and Johnny McGivern swung down to put up the bars after them.

He was a smiling boy, and he grinned at Laban. "I hear you're the hostler here. Well, there's a stage comin' through nigh on to noon, so you be set an' ready. Any chance to get some grub?"

"I'll ask ma," Laban replied with dignity, not sure how he should react to this free-talking stranger.

One of the older men was long and slim and red-headed, with red hair on the backs of his hands. "I'm Kris Mahler, son. This galoot sportin' the remains of a shiner is Conn Conagher. Shy clear of him, boy, he's got a burr under his saddle."

Conagher was a lean, dark man of about thirty-five, with black hair and mustache, and a stubble of beard. He wore a battered black hat, a shabby suit-coat and leather chaps. His boots were down at the heel, his gun scabbard worn, and the walnut grips looked as if they had seen much use.

Conagher looked at Laban quite seriously. "Don't you set much store by what Kris tells you, boy. I'm a right peace-loving man."

"Who gave you the black eye?" Laban asked.

"Nobody gave it to me, son," Conagher said. "I fought for it."

"That's the second black eye we've seen," Ruthie said. "Kiowa Staples had one, too."

When nobody replied to that, Ruthie added, "He says he's going to kill the man who gave it to him."

Conn Conagher said nothing, but Kris Mahler threw him a quick glance and said, "Little girl, I reckon your ma wants to see you."

"Ain't her fault," Johnny McGivern said. "If Kiowa said it, he said it, that's all!"

Evie Teale came out of the door, drying her hands on her apron. "Won't you gentlemen come in for a bite? There's been no stage, and the food is ready."

"I'd take that kindly," Mahler said. "Come on, Conn. Let's eat and ride."

Conn lingered. He studied the crude shelter and Laban watched him, fearful of his comment. After a while, Conn nodded. "That's a pretty good job, son. Did you do that all by yourself?"

"Yes, sir."

Conn glanced at him. "Sir. Now that's nice, right nice."

Conagher strolled over and took a closer look at the shelter. "It helps," he said, "if when you start laying on cover you put the bottom ones on first, then put the next row a mite higher with part of it overlapping. Helps the water to run off."

"Thanks," Laban said. He found himself liking the grim, dark-faced man, and the boy and man walked toward the cabin together. Outside the cabin Conn removed his coat and rolled up his sleeves to wash his hands and face, and then combed his black hair.

He turned, looking across the valley into the distance. "I like that," he said, gesturing toward the view. "Nothing like a wide-open country."

"We saw Indian tracks," Laban said.

Conagher stopped and looked at him, then tilted his hat brim down and studied the hills back of the cabin. "You got a rifle in there?"

"We've got a shotgun."

"That's good, but you'd better have a rifle too. When your pa gets here he'll most likely have one."

They went inside. During the meal Mahler did most of the talking, aided by Johnny McGivern. Evie was bright and gay, excited by the company and glad to be hearing some news, even though much of it concerned events and people of whom she knew nothing.

When the others had gone outside, Mahler lingered. "Your girl said something about Kiowa Staples threatening to kill the man he fought. Is that true?"

"Well, he did say it. He was just talking."

"Not Kiowa. His kind don't 'just talk.' He meant it."

"What happened?"

"Only careless talk. Kiowa'd had a couple of drinks and he bumped into Conn a time or two. I won't say it was a-purpose, but he was sure not tryin' to avoid it. They had words and I figure Kiowa was expectin' gunplay, only Conn belted him . . . knocked him down.

"They went around and around there for a while, but this here saddle tramp—Conagher, I mean—he's a mean one to tangle with, and he gave Kiowa a trimming."

"Will there be more trouble?"

"No tellin'. Conagher's a drifter. Never lights any place for long, I figure, and he may drift clean out of the country before the two of them meet . . . but he's just stubborn enough to stick around."

"Who is he?"

Mahler shrugged. "Wildy hired him for this job. He don't talk none about himself . . . does his share and a mite more, I'd say, and minds his own affairs. He goes his own way, and the way I'd see it he just don't give a damn—beggin' your pardon, ma'am."

From the window, as she washed dishes, Evie watched Conagher tightening his cinch. He seemed a strange, lonely man and her heart went out to him, although he seemed not to have noticed her. She was used to that. Men never had noticed her very much, and now that she was no longer a young girl they noticed her even less. She was not even sure that Jacob had noticed her, or that he gave much thought to what she cared about or what she dreamed. He had been looking for a steady woman who would care for his children and help him build a home in the western lands. There was no romance about Jacob Teale.

Yet what right had she to object to the way he was? She had been frightened before they met; her money was almost gone and she had no relatives. There was no place for her to go. Jacob was seeking help and she was seeking shelter, and both found what they wanted.

Now she had the two children and she did not shrink from the task of raising them; she had grown to love them both. But she was a woman, with a woman's love to give, and she needed someone reaching out for it. There was an emptiness within her, a yearning that must be fulfilled, a love that needed to be given.

She went to the door when the riders rode away, driving their small herd to the other stations to the westward. They stood there, she and Ruthie, watching them until even the dust was gone.

Laban had already gone back to his work. He was removing the pine and cedar boughs from the lean-to and re-laying them.

"It will be more waterproof if I lay the bottom rows first and let the next row overlap," he explained. "I don't know what I was thinking when I started it."

They were alone again, and the silence had come.

3

Conn Conagher tied his bandana over his mouth to keep out the dust of the drag. Once he turned to glance back toward the cabin, but it was already obscured by the dust behind the horses.

Hell of a thing, he said to himself, *leavin' a woman and two kids out there alone.* But even as he said it he knew that many a man had no choice. You took your chances in this country; some of them paid off and some did not.

He gave no thought to Kiowa Staples. The man had the name of a gunfighter, and he had killed a couple of men—one of them up at Tin-Cup, in Colorado, the other at Mobeete, in Texas. Conn Conagher had seen a good many who fancied themselves with guns, and had helped to bury at least one. They came and they went.

He rubbed the itchy stubble on his jaws and squinted through the dust. He had been figuring on drifting to Tucson, or maybe out to California. He had ridden for a couple of California outfits, and it beat fighting northers in Texas or New Mexico.

He wasn't getting any younger, and it was time he found himself a place to light. Twenty-two years now he'd spent on the hurricane deck of a bronc, and it was time he found himself a chair on the porch somewhere, or spent a winter at one of those fancy Colorado hotels.

Then he snorted with disgust. What was he thinking of? He couldn't even afford a new pair of boots. He was a thirty-dollar cowhand, and that was all he was likely to be.

They pushed the horses at a good pace, and although the sun was close to setting they kept on. The next station was not many miles off, and if they rode on in it would be to a warm fire and ready-made grub.

Kris Mahler dropped back to talk to Conagher. "What do you think? Shall we go on in?"

"Gettin' paid for the job, ain't we? Why waste time? We can make it short of midnight, and these mustangs won't suffer none. Drive 'em on in an' tomorrow they'll be fit as fiddles."

There were two men at Red Rock, but there was no evidence of it when the herd rounded into the station. McGivern rode over to the corral and opened the gate for the horses, who smelled the water in the trough and pushed in, eager to reach it.

Only when Mahler got down at the door did it open cautiously.

"Who's there?" came the question.

Conn Conagher yelled his answer. "It's an apostle with an epistle for you! Open up, you sod-busters and let a man in!"

The door creaked on its hinges and they saw the white undershirt of a man in his pants, holding a rifle. "Put your horses up, an' come on in. I'll set the coffee on the fire."

After turning his horse into the corral Conn followed the others in. He was tired and cold.

He nursed the cup of coffee in his stiff fingers. If he stayed in this country he'd have to rustle himself a sheepskin or buffalo coat, and he did not want to leave with Kiowa making war talk . . . he would like to see him first. Likely it was all talk, but you never knew.

Between cups, while waiting for the beans and corn-

pone, he pulled off his boots. There was another hole
in his socks. Reminded him of the cowpuncher who
went to wash his feet one spring and found two pairs of
socks he didn't know he had.

Conn picked up his cup again, and sipped the coffee
while staring into the fire. There was a world of comfort in a fire, and he'd looked into a sight of them,
round and about.

The station agent was a man of fifty or more, the
hostler older, yet they'd found a place to light. The
older you got the tougher it got. You felt the cold more,
and you didn't take to sleeping out on the ground so
much. A man that old should have himself a home, a
place to hang his hat while he waited for the sunset.

The waiting would not be bad if it was on a man's
own place, where he could watch his own cattle graze
and could live in some kind of peace. Conn turned his
foot sideways. The heels of his boots were run down
and the soles were growing thin. Lucky he was a rider
and not a walker or they'd last no time at all.

He'd never had a home that you could call a home.
His ma had died when he was four, and his pa had
gone off to help build railroads and had never come
back. His aunt and uncle had taken him in, but he'd
worked for it. Lord above, how he had worked! His
aunt always threw it up to him how his pa had never
come back . . . well, a lot of men went west who never
came back, and it wasn't their fault either.

And it didn't have to be Injuns. Cholera had done
for a lot of them, and starvation and thirst for a good
many more, and some had been killed by men like
Kiowa Staples, who were hunting a reputation. If you
got thrown from your horse out on the prairie alone, or
got caught in a stampede, gored by a longhorn, or
drowned swimming a river . . . there were a hundred
ways a man could die in this western country, and no-

body the wiser. It was likely the way he himself would end.

Somebody poured coffee into his cup and he muttered a thanks without looking up. His fingers were beginning to get warm. It beat all how this country could be hot in the daytime and could freeze up at night.

It was time he started hunting himself a place to last out the winter. He didn't have to feel in his jeans to know there was just two dollars there. Two lone silver dollars, and whatever he'd get out of this job—he'd have to rustle a job on one of these new cow outfits.

Twenty-two years . . . it was too long . . . and nothing ahead of him but a stiffening of muscles, growing tired a little sooner, finding it harder to keep warm. He'd driven spikes on the railroad, handled a cross-cut saw in a tie camp, helped to sink a shaft on a contract job, and helped to build a couple of mountain roads in Colorado. Then he'd driven a team over the Santa Fe, put in four years in the army in the War Between the States and got to be a sergeant. He had been wounded twice, escaped from Andersonville, and had fought Indians in Dakota and Wyoming. He'd gone up the trail from Texas three times, and had punched cows in Texas, the Arizona Territory, Nebraska, and Wyoming. It was a hard life, a bitter, lonely life after a fellow got beyond the kid stage.

When you were a youngster everything seemed easy, and life was forever. He'd spent a lot of time dreaming about girls, usually about one girl whose face kept changing, but who was always mighty in love with him, and he ready to die for her . . . only he never met her, somehow.

He'd never cared for the women on the Line, although he'd had his dealings with them. There'd been a girl he knew in a Missouri town where he drove some cattle . . . only she married a home guard there, and already had a baby boy when he came back up the trail. That had been just as well, because she wasn't his cup of tea . . . he'd tried to talk himself into it. And now he was thirty-five, with nothing but his chaps and his saddle, and womenfolks didn't cotton to a man with nothing who wasn't going anywhere.

These thoughts went through his mind as he ate his beans and some almighty tough meat, and sopped his corn bread in the gravy and settled back to drinking coffee. He was a coffee drinker, and he liked it black and bitter.

The trouble with him, he was thinking, was that the kind of a woman he fancied was hard to come by, and he wasn't likely to settle for less. He did not want a big, bustling, brassy woman; he wanted something dainty and feminine he could carry flowers to without her thinking he'd gone off his rocker. The womenfolks he met, at least the single ones, they were hunting a man with a wide stretch of land, with cows to his name and a ranch house with more than two rooms. Well, he could build the ranch house, if it came to that. He'd always been a fair hand with tools.

"What you goin' to do when you pay off, Conn?" Kris Mahler was asking. "You goin' to get drunk?"

"Ain't likely. I'm going to rustle me a job, someplace I can put my feet under the table for the rest of the winter."

"You goin' south?"

"No." He made the decision as he shaped the words. "I'm going to stay right here. In this here country somewhere."

"You got friends here?" Johnny asked.

"I got no friends anywhere. Only whiskey friends, and that kind don't stay by you. Seems like I been driftin' ever since I can remember."

"You seen a lot of country, they tell me."

"Me? I've punched cows from the Musselshell in Montana to the Rio Fuerte in Sonora, and all I got to show for it is saddle sores and savvy, and a thumb lost on the Brazos when I was tryin' for an extra turn around the horn and a fifteen-hundred-pound steer hit the end of the string. Took my thumb off, and me thirty miles from the ranch and twenty-two from town. I stubbed it against my shirt to hold down the bleeding and heated a brandin' iron—I cauterized it right there with a runnin' iron.

"Then I rode on the twenty-two miles to an Army-post town to let the doc look it over. He looks it over, and then he says, "You lost a thumb, boy." All of which I could have told him. Then he gave me a stiff drink of rye, had one himself, and cleaned her up a mite, stuck a bandage on it, and charged me four bits for the job."

Conn got up. "I'm for sleep. Where can I bed down?"

"Any place you can find to suit you, as long as it's on the floor."

Conn unrolled his two blankets and ground sheet. Then he straightened up. "Woman over east of here saw Injun tracks a few days back."

"I ain't seen any," the station agent said. "I figure she's imaginin' things."

Conn laid out his bed before he replied, and then he straightened up and slipped off his pants. "No, if she says she saw tracks, she saw 'em all right. That's a pretty steady woman yonder."

Long after the light was out Conn lay on his back, his hands clasped behind his head, staring up into the darkness, just thinking. There was water in the Mogollons, and a man might be able to make it up there, with a few head of stock.

At breakfast Johnny McGivern looked at him curiously. "What you goin' to do about Kiowa Staples?"

"*Do?* What's there to do? Ever'where you go, Buster, there's a Kiowa Staples, ever' town an' ever' cow outfit. If a man lets himself be bothered by such as them he ain't goin' far. I've seen them come and go. If he minds his own affairs, I'll mind mine. If he starts anything with me I'll just cloud up and rain all over him."

Conagher took his pay at the Plaza and recovered his own horse from the stage-line corral. He threw his beat-up saddle on the dun and rode down the street. He drew up at a saloon, tied his horse, and went in.

Mahler was there, and he greeted Conagher. "Have one on me. They've hired me to wrangle stock for 'em."

"Luck!" Conagher said, and took his drink. He tossed it down, giving the few men in the room a cool glance. "I'll buy one, and then I'm riding."

Mahler leaned closer. "Staples is in town."

"The hell with him."

Conagher rode to the store, only a few steps away, and bought himself a new rope, some coffee, a side of bacon, flour, dried fruit, and some odds and ends. Made up in a sack, it would ride easy behind his saddle.

Outside he threw it into position behind his saddle and was about to hang the coil of rope over the horn when he heard a step behind him. "All right, Conagher. This time it won't be fists."

It was Staples' voice, and Conn turned on one heel, swinging the tightly coiled rope in a sweeping blow that caught the gunman across the face. It was a brutal blow; the coiled rope was like iron and it caught Staples across the mouth and nose, knocking him staggering into the hitching rail.

Coolly, matter-of-factly, and without hurry, Conagher

swung the coil again, smashing him across the mouth as Staples clawed for his gun.

The gunman never had a chance. He had expected a gun battle or an argument—anything but this. Conagher stood wide-legged in front of him and, backing the gunman against the rail, he proceeded to beat him unmercifully with the swinging coil of rope.

No matter how Staples tried to turn, the rope was there to meet him. His nose was broken, his lips smashed to pulp, his cheeks and ears bloody, and when he finally got his gun out a sweeping blow with the coiled rope struck it from his hand into the dust.

At no time did Conagher seem hurried. He whipped Staples coldly, almost casually, as though it were of no importance. The crowd that gathered watched silently and in awe.

When Kiowa went to his knees, Conagher struck him one more swinging blow that knocked him into the dust, and then he said, "You better ride out of here, Staples. An' leave that gun alone. You ain't fit to handle one. And don't you cross my trail again. I don't like bein' braced by no tinhorn."

Picking up the gun, he shucked the cartridges from it and dropped them into his pocket, and dropped the gun into the water trough. Then he mounted up and rode out of town.

Kiowa Staples sat very still, sure of only one thing—that if he moved Conagher would come back. He sat there breathing in deep, shuddering gasps, the blood falling in slow drops from his nose and mouth.

Slowly the crowd filtered away, and when finally the beaten gunman staggered to his feet he fell back against the hitching rail and stood clutching it, his head hanging.

A trouble maker leaned over. "Kiowa, you want to borrow my gun?"

Staples turned his head and stared at the man blankly, then he straightened up and staggered away. He wanted only a horse. He wanted only to ride away, out of here.

4

When Jacob Teale had been gone for two months, Evie had her first doubts. Travel was hard, and he might have had to go further to find cattle he could buy, but he would surely have sent word. He would have written.

Jacob had never been a heedless man. He was not thoughtful about her needs, but he was a practical man who did whatever needed to be done. Somehow, had he been able, he would surely have sent word.

The supplies brought by the stage company had lasted well, and Evie had ordered again. She had even managed to save two dollars which she carefully put away.

It was Laban who worried her. He was working too hard, caring for the horses, getting them out to meet the stages, picketing them on grass to make the little hay they had last, and cutting wood for the house. She had tried to help, but he resented it, wanting to carry on by himself.

She saw no more of Kiowa Staples. Charlie McCloud had given her a brief account of what had happened. "Never saw anything like it," he said. "Staples came a-hunting trouble and Conagher gave it to him. It was as bad a whipping as a man ever got. Have you ever seen what a club forty-five feet of rope will make when it's in a tight coil? I can tell you one thing. Staples may take a shot at Conagher from ambush sometime, but he sure won't face him again.

"Kiowa never expected anything like that. He expected Conn to try to draw against him, but that swinging coil of rope just knocked him groggy. He'd been hit four or five times before he even had a chance to do anything, and Conagher never let him get set. I figure that's one would-be gunman who is cured."

It was hard to believe it of the quiet, rather gentle man she recalled. When she said as much, McCloud shrugged. "Mrs. Teale, I figure this Conagher's got a lot behind him. He ain't come to this of a sudden. He's a man who's had years of it to put the steel in him. He's seen a-plenty and he just ain't about to be bothered by any tinhorn who comes along the pike."

And then he repeated what someone else had said. "He's the kind you just don't push, Mrs. Teale. Reminds me of Billy Brooks over to Dodge. Billy was a gun-using marshal and a good one. In his first two or three months on the job he shot thirteen men . . . I don't mean he killed them all, but he was engaged in gunplay with them. Then he crossed horns with a tough old buffalo hunter named Kirk Jordan, and Kirk made Billy take water. He run Billy clean out of town.

"Any gunman who wants to build himself a reputation had best steer clear of men like Kirk Jordan or Conn Conagher, and a few others I could name. They just don't put up with foolishness."

The arrival of the stage was the big moment of the day, and when it was gone there was a time of clearing up and taking stock. The stage brought news, and there was talk of politics, gun-fighters, Indians, or range conditions.

When evening came Evie stood at the door and

looked far across the grass, scenting the wind from the distant ranges with its smell of hot grass and the fainter smell of cedar from the ridges beyond.

She never tired of looking out across the plain, nor of watching the tumbleweeds roll past when the wind blew strong, rolling along like brown, fat cart wheels across the open country. Sometimes she could count fifty or sixty at once, rolling away, stopping when the wind died, then rolling on again as the breeze rose.

Where did they go? Was there a fence out there somewhere where they could hang up and rest? Was there a wall of brush? A forest? A mountain range? Or did they just roll on and on forever, clear around the world, maybe?

She could watch the wide plain from the window near which she cooked and washed the dishes; she could see the ever-changing light upon it, the cloud shadows, and sometimes the suggestion of movement out there beyond the range of her sight.

How far was it across that plain? She did not know, and she never asked, for she did not want it reduced to miles. To her it went on forever . . . it was like a vast sea.

"I wish we had more to read," Laban said one night. "I need schoolin'."

"Yes, we all need more to read." She rested her hands from sewing. "I will speak to Mr. McCloud. He may be able to find some newspapers or magazines."

She took up the sewing again, although her fingers were tired, and her eyes ached. "Until then, Laban, you can read the land."

"The land?"

"Look upon the land, Laban—there are stories everywhere. Study the sky and the trees, the tracks of animals and the way the birds fly. You can learn things no book will ever teach you."

"I saw the track of a snake yesterday," Ruthie said. "It was near the spring."

"You be careful," Laban warned. "There's rattlers around."

When they stopped talking they could hear the coyotes. And then suddenly there was a rushing and plunging from the corral.

"Indians!" Laban was up, running for the shotgun.

Evie had put down her sewing and got to her feet. She went to the door and took up the still lighted lantern standing there. Abruptly, she swung the door wide and lifted the lantern.

The ranch yard was crowded with horses, and among them, striking at the bars of the corral gate, was a magnificent wild stallion.

He swung toward the light as it fell across the horses, and he blew shrilly, in challenge as well as in astonishment. He was not beautiful, but stocky and strong, with an ugly head and teeth that flashed as he rolled his eyes toward the light. His mane was tangled and wild, and he swung from the corral and faced the light, bobbing his head and pawing the hard earth with fierce, challenging strokes. Then he swung suddenly and, nipping at the nearest horse, drove his herd from the yard.

For a long time she stood there, listening to the receding pound of their hoofs, and then she went to the corral.

The horses in the corral were wild and frightened, drawn by the wildness of the mustang stallion, but shuddering with fear, too. She talked to them calmly, replacing the one bar that had been knocked from the gate. She had known there were wild horses out there on the plains, but these were the first she had seen. For a long time she remembered that stallion, and the wild look in his eyes as he stared at her.

The cabin door, when she closed and barred it, was a comforting thing.

The days grew colder. Evie spent much of her time out with the children, gathering fuel from the hillsides. Ancient cedars had fallen, leaving their gray, gnarled, and twisted limbs on the broken rocks of the steep slope. They dragged them down to the cabin, picking up twigs, branches . . . all that could be found.

Sometimes Laban or Ruthie would saddle Nathan, their appaloosa gelding, and ride out to rope and drag home tree trunks or heavy limbs from farther away, building a slowly growing pile of fuel against the coming cold.

It was on a frosty morning that Charlie McCloud turned the stage into the yard and swung down to open the door for the passengers. There were four that morning, two ladies from the East—and they were ladies—well gotten up for the time and the place, and two men who looked tough and capable. Both wore business suits, wide hats and boots, and the taller of the two wore a United States marshal's badge.

Charlie reached into the boot and took out an armful of newspapers and magazines, and a couple of books. "Some of them are beat-up, Mrs. Teale," he said, "but there's some readin' for you."

Inside the house, Evie quickly put food on the table, and then asked the women, "Would you prefer tea? I have some."

"Would you, please?" said the older one. "I mean, if it isn't asking too much. The coffee . . . it's so *strong*."

"They like it strong out here. They say if you can't float a horseshoe on it the coffee is too weak."

When she had tea on the table she went to the cupboard and got out a plate of cookies.

McCloud stared at them. "Mrs. Teale, you been

holdin' out on us. Those are the first cookies I've seen you make."

"I didn't know you liked them. I often make doughnuts, too."

"Better not let it get around," Charlie said, "or you'll have half the cowboys in the Territory hangin' around . . . ridin' for miles to get here."

"You will have to forgive us," Evie said to the ladies. "The place is rather primitive. Next year we hope to add to the cabin so we will have more room."

"I love your view," the younger woman said. She was no more than nineteen, with large blue eyes and long lashes. "Mrs. Teale, I am Lucy Baker, and this is my aunt, Celestine Scott. We are from Philadelphia, and were going to Prescott. We're looking for my brother."

"He lives in Prescott?"

"No, that was the last address we had for him. That . . . that was two years ago."

"Two *years?* The way people travel in this country he might be anywhere. What is his name?"

"Scott Baker . . . you'd know him easily. He's tall, and has dark, tight curls. There's a small scar on his cheek bone, and he has a beautiful smile. He's always making fun . . . they used to say he was wild, but that was just his way."

"If he comes by, I'll speak to him," Evie said. "You leave me your address."

Suddenly she noticed the tall man with the marshal's badge. His expression was odd, and he was stirring his coffee very busily. The other man was looking down at his plate.

The marshal looked up then and said, "Miss, if you want to stop around the Plaza—that's the next town down the line—you might run into him. I couldn't say for sure, but there's a man around there called Curly— he seems to fit the description."

Evie's head came up sharply and her eye caught that of the marshal, who slowly shook his head.

Scott Baker . . . curly hair . . . *Curly Scott*! She had heard Charlie McCloud speak of him. Curly Scott was one of the Parnell gang, wanted by Wells Fargo for stage holdups. There were five of them, sometimes six, and they were a tough outfit.

Smoke Parnell was a lean, lath of a man with a long, hatchet face who had come west from the Bald Knob country of Missouri. He was a dead shot with a rifle, and a fair hand with a short gun. He had come into the Territory from Nevada and was suspected of a stage holdup in Black Canyon, south of Prescott. The gang was also wanted for raiding several mining operations, and for at least one killing during the course of a robbery.

"Your brother been out here long?" the marshal asked.

"Oh, he came out about three years ago," Lucy Baker said. "He wanted to leave school and try mining for a while. He had a mine somewhere in the Mogollons." She pronounced the word with an emphasis on the "goll" and not as it was spoken in the area, as "Muggy-owns." "I don't know how successful he has been, but when we did not hear from him for so long, we were worried . . . and my aunt wanted to come west, anyway."

Evie poured her own cup of tea and sat down at the table while the marshal and his companion went outside to talk to Charlie McCloud. She was starved for the companionship of women, and she longed to talk to them. While she was taking in their clothes her heart went out to them as she thought of the shock it would be for them to learn that Curly Scott was an outlaw.

"I love it here," she said suddenly. "I think there is

something here, something more than all you see and feel . . . it's in the wind.

"Oh, it is very hard!" she went on. "I miss women to talk to, I miss the things we had back East—the band concerts, the dances. The only time when we see anyone is like now, when the stage comes. But you do not know what music is until you have heard the wind in the cedars, or the far-off wind in the pines. Someday I am going to get on a horse and ride out there"—she pointed toward the wide grass before them—"until I can see the other side . . . if there is another side."

"What about the Indians? Aren't you afraid of them?" Lucy Baker asked.

"So far we haven't seen any. We hear rumors. The Apaches are raiding to the south of us, but so far they haven't come up here. We will have to face that when the time comes."

Long after they were gone Evie could hear the sound of their voices. At the end the two women had talked of clothes and fashions, of the theater, and of schools. She would stop often and look out over the plains, which grew blue and then a dusky purple as evening came, and she would try to remember all that had been said.

She wished she could have warned them about Curly. They would stop in the Plaza, but the marshal would be there, too, and if Curly heard they were there he would ride in to meet them.

Early the following morning Laban had gone to feed the stock. Ruthie had gone with him, and Evie was finishing the morning dishes. She dried her hands on her apron, and almost automatically her eyes lifted to the hills.

She saw the Indians at once. There were a dozen of them, and they were coming single file down the mountain. There were no squaws among them, just warriors, and they were stripped for action.

"Laban!" she called. "Come to the cabin! Both of you! Come quickly!"

Laban straightened up and started to protest, then he caught Ruthie by the shoulder. "Let's go," he said.

She jerked her shoulder free. "Don't be so bossy!" she said.

"Ruth!" Evie spoke sharply. "Come . . . *now!*"

Ruthie started to speak to assert her independence, but Laban just scooped her up in his arms and carried her to the cabin, kicking and arguing.

He dropped her at the door and she started to run back. "What is it, ma!" Laban asked.

"Indians," Evie said. "They are coming down the mountain. You'd better come in, Ruth."

Ruthie turned sharply, looked up at the mountain, and then, her face suddenly white, she ran into the cabin. Laban stopped to gather an armful of wood. he came in and went to the back of the cabin closed the strong wooden shutters. There were loop holes in the walls through which they could fire. Evie put the bar close to the door, but left the door open part way.

Her heart was pounding and her lips were dry. "Laban," she said, "they must not know we are alone here, and they must not know we are frightened."

"All right, ma."

He was standing in the middle of the room, looking around. There was nothing that remained to be done.

"They will try to take the horses," he said.

"Yes. We must stop them if we can."

The Indians rode suddenly into the yard, and drew up when they saw her standing in the door. Laban was poised behind it, ready to slam it shut and drop the bar.

"What is it you want?" Evie asked.

"Grub," one of them said. "You give us grub."

"I am sorry. I have none to spare."

Ruthie took up the rifle Charlie McCloud had brought to them and slid the muzzle through a loop hole.

"You give us grub or we take horses. We take cow."

"Ride on," Evie ordered, "ride on now! We do not want trouble, but you must not come here like this. I do not like threats. Go now."

They looked at her. Their horses shifted position, and one Indian rode slowly around the cabin.

She stood very still, the shotgun held in the fold of her dress, concealed by it. She sensed they were not sure. They could see the muzzle of one gun, and she seemed very confident.

One of the Indians turned his pony and started for the horse corral.

"Tell that man to leave the horses alone," she said clearly.

Suddenly, they charged.

What warned her, she never knew. Perhaps it was the tensing of muscles before the horses lunged. They were not forty feet from the door when they started.

She lifted the shotgun and fired from the hip . . . there was no time to raise it further. Then she stepped back so quickly she almost tripped, and Laban slammed the door and dropped the bar.

Bodies crashed against the door and she opened the loop hole in the heavy door and fired the shotgun through it.

She heard a scream, then a scattering. Laban leaped to take the rifle from Ruthie and fired almost without aiming.

"You got one, ma," Ruthie said. "You killed one of them. There's another bleeding something awful."

Laban not only had the rifle, but was a good shot. He was watching the horses while Ruthie and Evie moved from loop hole to loop hole to see what was happening.

All was quiet outside. The one Indian lay sprawled in the yard, a pool of blood under him and around him. The shotgun blast had caught him not more than twenty feet off, for he was coming at them when she fired. The heavy charge of buckshot must have nearly cut him in two.

Suddenly Laban fired the rifle again.

The corral stood out in the open, and it was not easy to approach it without being seen.

"Ma," Laban said, "it's almost time for the stage. They'll be here when it comes."

The stage . . . she had forgotten about the stage.

"Ruthie," she said, "go up in the loft and keep a watch out on the road. When you see it coming, call down to Laban and he can start shooting."

"What if there's nothing to shoot at?" Laban asked.

"Shoot anyway. It will warn them on the stage. Shoot where you think you'd be if you were an Indian."

Going to the fireplace, she made coffee, put the bean pot close to the fire to warm, and then sliced some meat. The chances were the stage would go right on through, but if they did stop, they must have warm food and hot coffee—above all, they would want coffee.

From time to time she peered through the loop holes, but there was nothing stirring. All was still, scarcely a breath of air moving. She could see sunlight on the grass out in front, the horses standing in the corral, and the view down the trail toward the Plaza, miles away. Within the cabin it was shadowed and quiet, the shutters closing out the light except the little that filtered through around them.

The stage was due by now. The passengers would be stiff and tired from the long ride in cramped quarters. Charlie or Ben Logan, who drove alternate, would be up on the box. He would be right out in the open and a perfect target. Evie was hoping there were no women aboard.

She checked the loads in the shotgun. She was frightened, but she knew what she must do. How many Indians there were she did not know . . . she thought she had seen a dozen, although there might have been twice as many. The dead one still lay in front of the house, and at least one had been wounded, the one Ruthie had seen with the bloody leg might have been on the porch when she fired through the loop hole. And Laban might have hit one.

The minutes went slowly by. She poured a cup of coffee for herself and one for Laban, who never drank coffee except on the coldest days.

"They're still out there, ma," Laban said. "I saw a magpie fly up just now. Something scared him, and the horses kind of shied, too."

Where was the stage?

Suddenly Ruthie called out, "Ma! It's comin'! The stage is comin'!"

Laban fired. The roar of the gun seemed unnaturally loud after the long silence in the shuttered cabin. Instantly he fired again. And then they saw the stage.

The team was running wild, and the driver lay slumped over the seat; how he was staying up there on the jolting, bounding stage was more than she could guess. She saw the team charging toward the cabin, and suddenly the driver sat up, swinging the horses right at the door.

Evie ran to the door and took down the bar. The team swung toward the door and the stage almost crashed against the side of the building, then stopped.

Evie swung the door open as two men and a woman almost fell from the stage. One of the men was dragging another one down. The driver—it was Ben Logan—fell into the room, his chest and one arm bloody. He clutched a .44 Colt and he paused one instant to fire before they slammed the door shut.

"Hit us about three mile up," he said, "around the Point. I figure we got a couple, but they hit us hard."

He staggered back and almost fell to a bench by the table, resting his gun hand on it.

The two active and able men, after dragging the wounded man inside, had gone at once to loop holes. There was almost steady firing now, and the room was filled with gun smoke.

"What kind of a roof you got, ma'am?" one of the men asked. "I didn't notice when we came in."

"It's a pole roof, covered with earth."

"Thank God for that! They can't set it afire."

The shooting slowed, then stopped.

The other man, short and stocky with a square, determined face, turned to Logan. "Ben, we've got to get that stage moved. They'll set it afire and burn the cabin."

"It's stone," Evie said.

"Makes no difference. They'll burn down the door and fire through the opening. Anyway, the smoke might do for us."

"The horses are still hitched," Ben said, "but I can't hold a rein."

The woman had been kneeling beside the wounded man, gently unbuttoning his vest and shirt. Evie went to her. "If we could get him on the bed—"

The woman looked up. She was scarcely more than a girl, with a round, pretty face. "We'd better not move him. He might be gut-shot."

The rough term from her lips was startling. Evie started to speak, then she realized what the woman probably was.

"Yes, yes, of course," she said. "There's hot water

on the fire and we have bandages. I'm afraid I don't know much about wounds."

"I do," the girl said practically. "I've seen a good many. I've lived in some shooting towns."

The stocky man was easing the door open, peering out. "One of the horses is down. He'll have to be cut from the harness first."

"Then cut him," Logan said. "There's no time to spare, man."

He tossed a bowie knife to the man at the door, who hesitated only a moment, then slipped out and went to his knees. Rising quickly, he slashed, then slashed again. The bowie knife had a heavy blade and was razor sharp. Seizing the whip, he lashed the nearest horse and the animal leaped, impelling the others. In an instant they were gone, careening across the yard, running down an Indian who sprang up suddenly from behind a cedar log.

The man who had done the cutting lunged for the door and tripped, and then was dragged inside as several bullets drummed on the door or ricocheted from the rock walls. And then again there was silence.

The girl had gone from the wounded man on the floor to Ben Logan. Working with smooth skill, she cleaned and then dressed his wounds.

Outside there was neither sound nor movement. The day wore on, the heat of the afternoon changing to the coolness of evening.

"What do you think, Ben?" the square-faced man asked Logan. "Will they stay and fight, or will they pull out?"

Ben Logan shrugged. "I figure they'll pull out. No Injun wants to fight a losin' battle, and they've lost more men today than in many a fight with the Army. I figure they'll try to get that dead one out yonder, and they may try for the horses, but they're likely to go."

After a moment he added, "They can count, good as you or me, and they know there's four, five guns in here, and we're behind a stone wall. They aren't out to win no medals."

It was a long, slow evening, and a longer, slower night. Several times, just to keep the Indians away, one of them fired a rifle along the side of the corral. It was a moonlit night and from the cabin the front of the corral and both sides were covered easily. Only the back of the corral could not be observed.

At daybreak the horses were still there, the body of the dead Indian was gone, and by ten o'clock they knew the siege had been lifted.

"Don't worry none," Logan said. "When the stage doesn't reach the Plaza they'll come huntin' us."

And they did . . . a party of forty horsemen, heavily armed.

5

The Apaches had come and gone, and they had left no scars on the landscape. Those who had attacked were a small renegade band who had come over the border from Mexico, from their hide-aways in the far-off Sierra Madres.

Evie Teale looked out over the brown grass of autumn, and thought of the Apaches. Only a week had gone by since the day the men rode in from the Plaza, but it seemed an age ago. Things had such a way of passing here and leaving no mark upon the land—people, events, storms, troubles.

But the Apaches had left a mark upon her, and upon Laban and Ruthie. From now on they would be more cautious, more wary, more aware that it could happen to them. But the attack had also left them stronger, in that they had faced an enemy and they had survived.

Evie Teale suddenly became aware of something else. For the first time she was at peace here, really at peace. She had believed the land was her enemy, and she had struggled against it, but you could not make war against a land any more than you could against the sea. One had to learn to live with it, to belong to it, to fit into its seasons and its ways.

The land was a living thing, breathing with the wind, weeping with the rain, growing somber with clouds or gay with sunlight.

When she had come to this place she had looked aghast upon desolation. Now the cabin no longer looked out of place, it no longer looked like something dropped alongside the way, for it had become a part of the landscape, as she had.

As she had. . . . She thought of that, and knew that it was true, and that it had been the sun and shadow on the grass out there which had first won her; but now she must do something herself, she must not leave it to the land alone.

"Laban . . . Ruthie . . . we're going to make a flower bed. We're going to plant some flowers."

They looked at her, surprised, but eager, anticipating. "We'll dig up some prairie flowers and plant them alongside the door," she said.

"Laban, you have to start it. Take your shovel and dig up a flower bed on each side of the door. From the corners of the cabin to the doorstep, and about four feet deep.

"Ruthie, you and I will go look for flowers. We'll get some daisies, and there's Indian paintbrush. . . . Come on!"

By the time they returned with a basket filled with carefully dug-up plants, Laban had the earth spaded up, raked, and watered ready for the planting.

"We should plant some trees," Evie said. "We've got water enough, and there's some young cottonwoods down by the creek."

It was dusk before they settled where the trees would be planted so that they would offer shade for the cabin and at the same time would not be in the way of the stages.

Often, after the children were in bed, Evie walked out in front of the cabin to look at the stars and to feel the wind. These were the lonely hours, when at last she could let down from the work of the day, when she could stand there and feel the wind touch her hair, when she could look at the bright, silent stars, and hear a coyote's plaintive cry come from far out on the plain.

Behind her the windows would show a faint light from her lantern, for the fire would be banked for the night, the coal-oil light would be out or turned low.

She could hear a faint stirring among the horses in the corral, and sometimes one would stamp or blow dust from his nostrils.

Jacob was gone. . . .

Now she accepted the fact. How or why he had gone she had no idea, but somehow he had been killed or had died or been injured in some terrible way. That he might have simply gone off and left them she did not for a moment consider. Jacob was too much a man of duty, and both his place and his children meant too much to him.

She had never been sure if he loved her, for he was not a tender man. In the few moments when he had approached tenderness he had seemed oddly uncomfortable, yet she felt that in his own way that he did care for her. He was simply one of those silent millions who have never really learned how to express what they feel, or somehow seem to find it indelicate to do so.

And she had needed love. She had needed tenderness. She was frightened and she was alone, and the romance she had needed so desperately, of which she had dreamed so long, was simply not in him to give.

This was the second time that death—for somehow she felt sure that Jacob was dead—had left her alone. First, it had been her father. Suddenly she was alone in a strange place and her father was dead; but he had taken from her more than a father, more than financial support—he had taken her dreams with him.

He had always been filled with plans—wild, impractical plans they might be, but plans, dreams . . . and a goal. He had always had that, and as swiftly as one faded away he was busy with another, and his stories as well as his dreams had fed her own dreaming. Always, somewhere in the offing there was a Prince Charming, a someone who needed her, someone who was young and handsome, and filled with romance.

When her father died she lost her dreams. There was nothing of the Prince Charming about Jacob Teale, but he was a rock to which she could cling, and she had been frightened. With no money, no home, and no chance even to work, she had accepted his offer of marriage.

Now she was alone again, yet not quite alone, for there were the children and they needed her. They needed her as much as she needed them. She had them, and she had this place; without them she would again be where she had been, a woman alone in a harsh world where there was no place for a woman alone.

The coolness of the night held a hint of distant rain. Something far out upon the grass stirred, and she heard the whisper of sound. She stood a moment longer, and then she went back to the cabin and let herself in, barring the door behind her.

A moment then, she listened, hearing the breathing in the loft above. She looked around at the shadowed room, lighted only by the lantern and a faint flickering from the fire.

A double bed, a table, some benches, a chair . . . the pots and pans shining upon the wall or near the fireplace, the hard-packed earth floor . . . Would she ever have a plank floor, now that Jacob was gone?

She went to her carpetbag, the repository of the few things she had brought with her when she came to Jacob, and took out a thin volume of poetry. For an hour she read, then stared into the fire for a long time. Her loneliness was with her always; only the hours when she was most busy gave her respite, and each stage she awaited with a half-conscious longing, a hope that someone, or something special would come for her.

Six months had gone by since Jacob Teale had ridden away, and she found herself hard put to remember his features. She remembered his square-shouldered dignity, his quiet, somewhat stern manner; and whenever she thought of him she found herself feeling guilty that she did not mourn him. But when she remembered him now he was like a stranger.

The following day Charlie McCloud brought in the stage, and there were no passengers, so he lingered, drinking coffee with her.

"Mrs. Teale," he said abruptly, "you ought to find

yourself a man. You're too fine a woman to go to waste out here like this."

"Mr. Teale has only been gone six months, Mr. Mc-Cloud. I think it is rather too soon to—"

"Nonsense!" he interrupted. "You know as well as I do that something's happened to him. Mrs. Teale, this here is a violent land, and I've helped bury two, three men whose names nobody knew . . . it happens all the time.

"A man can get throwed by his horse out there on the plains and he can die of thirst before he can get anywhere. That's why they hang horse thieves, ma'am, because out here if you take a man's horse you may have taken his life along with it.

"It's a sight easier to die out here than to live. It doesn't have to be Injuns or outlaws. Now, you take your husband. I've asked around, passed the word along the stage line for any information about him or his horse. Neither of them seems to have been seen by anybody. I'd say that was pretty good evidence that they ran into trouble somewhere together.

"There was a flood on the Rio Grande shortly after he left here, and heavy rains over east of here, too. He may have tried to swim a river or take a short cut across country somewhere. You'd better count yourself a widow, Mrs. Teale."

"Perhaps you are right, Mr. McCloud. I would not say it to anyone but a good friend, but I *am* lonely, and sometimes when we are alone here, I am frightened; but even if I was sure Mr. Teale was dead, I still would know of no one I'd be interested in."

"Well," he said, "you deserve yourself a good man, and I'd surely say I'd be the last to advise you to latch onto the first saddle tramp who comes along. But you see, Mrs. Teale, the stage line . . . well, they want to put in their own station out west of here, four or five miles. I know you've been making a little off feeding us, but that time's about up, ma'am. I don't see how you're going to make it without the stages stopping here."

She had known it was coming, of course. From the first, the stage company had planned to build their own place, and she knew her small cabin was not adequate.

"This is all we have, Mr. McCloud, and we must do the best we can. Mr. Teale had hoped to have a herd started by this time, but I've had no money to buy cattle."

Charlie McCloud put down his cup. "Mrs. Teale, I've got me an idea. There's a herd a-passin' through here, and when they come you should go talk to the trail boss. Now, this here is a mixed herd, and they've got some long, dry drives ahead, I'll bet you you could get some calves.

"You'd have to wean 'em, most likely, but you've got that milk cow. No trail boss likes to be bothered with calves, and where they don't have a wagon to carry 'em in they just let 'em lay."

Suddenly his eyes began to twinkle. "Ma'am, I'll tell you what you do. Make up a big batch of them doughnuts. The average cow-poke would sell his soul for a doughnut. You make up a batch, have a couple of gallons of coffee handy, and you feed those cowboys and tell them if they have any fresh-dropped calves you'd like to have them. They know those calves aren't going to last out any desert crossing. You're liable to pick up four or five, maybe more."

She got up. "Thanks, Mr. McCloud, for what you've told me. Thank you very much."

He rose, hesitating a moment. "Don't you be forgetting. You keep your eye out for a good man, and latch onto him. There's a-plenty running around who are no good. You need you a good, steady man."

"Mr. McCloud, if I marry again it will be for love, and only for love. I don't care what comes. A woman deserves some happiness, Mr. McCloud, and I've had precious little, but I can't leave this place. It is all we have."

She knew his advice was good, for she had already seen how hungry travelers were for any kind of baking, and for doughnuts in particular. The cattle would be coming through soon and she was going to gamble all she had at hand on a chance of success.

With Ruthie helping, and Laban gathering additional firewood, she went to work to bake the doughnuts and prepare for a cowboy invasion. As she worked she considered the future. If she could get several calves it would be a start, at least, and Bess would be dropping a calf before the winter was over.

Before the herd came in sight they could hear the cattle bawling, and the herd was a big one.

Two men riding point swung away from the herd as it prepared to bed down for the night, and rode up to the cabin. Evie met them at the door, with Ruthie and Laban at her side.

The first was a lean, broad-shouldered man with a walrus mustache, and the second an older man, leaner still and stooped in the shoulders.

"Are you the lady who bakes the bear sign?"

"Bear sign?" Evie was puzzled. "Do you mean doughnuts?"

"Yes'm, reckon I do. We heard tell you was the best all-fired doughnut maker this side of the Mississippi, and that you'd set us up to doughnuts."

"Come on in," Evie said. "I've coffee on."

The two men swung down and went inside, hats in hand. Both men were armed, both were dusty and tired-looking. They seated themselves and she put out a tray of doughnuts and filled their cups.

After a few minutes of silent eating, the first man looked up. "I am John Catlin, ma'am, and this gent here ridin' herd on me is my uncle, Sam Catlin. We hear tell how you'd like some calves."

"I can't afford to buy them," Evie confessed. "I'd heard that when you were driving a mixed herd calves could be a trouble. I thought perhaps you might have one or two that you want to be rid of."

"That we do," the younger Catlin said. "They'd never make it across the desert anyway, and they'd be a trouble on the drive. As a matter of fact, I've got six head, a week to three weeks old, and we've lost a couple back yonder that couldn't keep up.

"Ma'am, we'd be pleased for you to have them, but I'm afraid it will cost you. We've got nine or ten hungry cowhands just a-sawin' at the bit to get over here."

"Send them, and you're welcome any time, whether you have calves or not, as long as the flour holds out."

An hour later she had five hungry cowhands around the table, and the way the doughnuts vanished was something to see, but they had brought with them six calves, all white-face, and along with them a cow.

"She's a mite old," Catlin said, "and likely this here's her last calf. I doubt whether she'd make it over the desert, so you're welcome."

Evie Teale stared at the cow. If it was more than five years old she was badly mistaken, and it looked to be in excellent shape, but she offered no comment beyond her thanks. The following morning when the herd moved out, the chuck wagon stopped by the house to fill its barrels with fresh water.

It was not until they were gone that Ruthie came running into the cabin. "Ma! Come look!"

On the doorstep was a hundred-pound sack of flour, fifty pounds of sugar, a sack of rice and one of beans, with a small package of dried fruit.

On top of them was a torn piece of canvas on which somebody had written, "With the thanks of the 2-C."

The Two Bar C was gone, but they would not be forgotten, and they had left behind them another legacy not lightly to be dismissed. Where the herd had bedded down there were cow chips enough for many a fire.

Evie Teale prepared for the next stage, and watched the sky. It was colder now, and the sky looked gray and lowering. They must work hard to gather fuel for the winter. It was surely on the way.

The wind was picking up, and the tumbleweeds were starting to roll. Soon they would be rolling off to the south in unnumbered legions. She counted those she could see rolling.

"... eight ... nine ... ten ... eleven ... twelve ..."

After that there was no use in counting, for they rolled away across the vast plain like an army of skirmishers—scattered out, moving forward, pausing, and then moving again.

"I wonder where they go," Laban said, watching them.

"I don't know, Laban. Maybe they just never stop. Maybe they just keep on rolling forever."

"They hang up against corrals sometimes, or fences."

"There are not many fences out here," Ruthie said, "but when we came West I saw a great bank of them against some willows and cottonwoods . . . remember? They were piled up as high as a house."

Again that night, when the children were asleep, Evie walked out in the moonlight.

The plain was stark and lonely, the stars shone unbelievably bright wherever the clouds broke for them to be seen. The wind whipped her skirt, and she saw one of the silent riders of the wind roll by not very far away.

Maybe . . . off to the south somewhere . . . maybe there was somebody down there as lonely as she was, somebody whose thoughts reached out into the emptiness of the night, longing, yearning, alone.

6

Conn Conagher came down out of the Mogollons riding a line-back dun. He had a healing scar over his right ear and a drawn look about him that showed even under the thick stubble of black beard. His blanket roll was tied behind his saddle and two rifles were tied across it. His own rifle was in its scabbard.

The Horse Springs stage station looked wind-blown and bleak when he rode in, huddled in his thin coat. He rode up to the station warily, like a man expecting trouble.

Two horses were tied at the hitching rail, both of them cow ponies wearing Ladder Five brands.

Conn glanced at the brands and muttered to his horse, "Now, there's a rustler's brand if ever I saw one. A Ladder Five will cover almost anything."

He tied his horse and went up the steps to the store's porch, then he opened the door and stepped in. There was a fire glowing in the stove, and three men sat around it. The storekeeper was arranging stock on the shelves.

Conn went up to the stove and warmed his hands. "Cold out there," he commented.

"Too cold."

"Makes a man wonder what he did with his summer's

wages," Conn continued. "Don't know anybody around who is looking for a hand, do you?"

"Can't say I do." The speaker was a square-built man in a buckskin jacket and battered hat. He wore moccasins rather than boots.

The other two looked like hard cases. Both were young, lean, and wiry, with a reckless cast to their features and a half-taunting expression that Conagher had seen many times before. These men were trouble, and trouble was the last thing he wanted right now.

He walked over to the counter. "Mister," he said, "I am in a swapping mood. I want one of them sheepskin coats and some gloves. Maybe a pair of Levis and some .44 ca'tridges."

"What have you got to swap? I usually do a cash-on-the-barrel-head business."

"I've got a couple of Winchesters," Conagher said. "I'll get 'em."

He went out, untied the two rifles, and brought them into the store. "They'll stand cleaning," he said.

The storekeeper took them in his hands, turned them over, tried the action, and looked down the barrel of each one. "Unusual thing," he commented, "a man wanting to swap off rifles, two of them."

"They belonged to a pair of Indians," Conagher said. "They jumped me up in the Mogollons. There were three of them. We had quite a go-around there for a few minutes."

The man in buckskin commented, "Three *Apaches?* You're lucky you've got your hair."

"Well, I seen a rabbit up ahead . . . maybe a hundred yards ahead. He was hoppin' along easy-like across the trail when he suddenly took off back the way he came, so I sort of figured there was something in the brush alongside the trail that scared him.

"If they were Indians they'd likely seen me, scouted

ahead to lay for me, and likely they were watching me now, so I pulled up and got down and picked up my horse's hoof—like it was giving me trouble.

"I hunted around for a rock, hit at the shoe a couple of times, then threw it down and picked up another, dropped it, and stepped over to the side of the trail, as if I was hunting a bigger rock. Then I ducked into the brush and sneaked up on 'em.

"Just about the time I got close they began to wonder what had become of me, so one of them craned his neck up out of the brush for a better look and he saw me. He was surprised, but I wasn't. He wasn't any more than thirty feet off, but when I commenced shooting I dusted the brush all around him and two Indians broke from cover, one of them dragging a wounded leg."

"So you nailed him," one of the cowhands said.

"No, I figured I had him, all right, so I let drive at the other one and dropped him. When I looked around for the wounded one, he was gone."

"Did you hunt him down?"

Conagher gave the cowhand a glance. "Mister, nobody but a fool goes into the rocks after a wounded Apache."

"How'd you get the rifles, then?"

"Well, I laid there a piece, and then I got over into the brush where I'd killed the first one, and I latched onto his rifle and ammunition. No use leaving it for some other Indian to kill with. Then I edged around until I could see the last Indian I shot, and with a long stick I pulled his rifle to me. Then I went back to my horse and lit a shuck out of there."

"I'll swap," the storekeeper said, "and I'll add a box of .44's for them you used up in the fight. Most of the Apaches around here are good people, and the Zunis north of us are no trouble makers, but it's them south-of-the-border 'Paches who keep raiding up here that give us trouble. They attacked the stage station down the line where that woman—Teale's her name —runs it."

Conn Conagher looked up sharply. "They didn't kill her?"

"She made a fight of it, she and them youngsters. Then the stage came in, all bloodied up, but amongst them they fought 'em off."

Conagher tried on a sheepskin coat, then another. Satisfied, he put the boxes of shells in the pockets and picked up the gloves and the jeans.

"Might as well set and have coffee," the storekeeper said. "You ain't goin' far tonight."

"Thanks. I'll move on."

The man in buckskin followed him outside, leaning on the hitching rail while Conagher tightened the cinch. "Where was you in the Mogollons?" he asked. "I'm a-headed up thataway."

"My guess would be you knew them pretty well," Conagher said. "What is it you want to know?"

The man in buckskin glanced over his shoulder. "I got me a little stand over on the Negrito. I was wonderin' if you'd been around thataway, and if you'd seen any Injun sign."

"I came down through Sheep Basin," Conagher said, "and I saw no Indian sign." He straightened up and rested his hands on the saddle. His eyes smiled a little, and he said, "I did see some other sign over on Beaverdam."

The man in buckskin flushed a little, then grinned. "Like I figured, you've got savvy," he said. "Those two in there . . . I don't cotton to 'em. I'd as soon they didn't know where I hole up."

"I'll do no talkin'. Ain't none of my affair." He held out a hand. "Name's Conagher. I'm ridin' the grub line whilst huntin' a job."

"If you don't find anything come on back to Beaverdam. There's wolves up there, bear oncet in a while, and a few beaver. A man can make out on deer if he likes venison. I live off the country, make up a few furs to bring out. My name is Chip Euston."

He came around the horses. "Watch yourself with those two in there. That whole Ladder Five is a salty crowd and they don't care whose stock they brand."

"Who are they?"

"Hi Jackson and Pete Casuse. They drifted in here from the Neuces country."

"Likely I'll never see them again. I'm driftin'."

But when he looked back from a distance of about half a mile, he saw the two men standing in front of the store, staring after him.

Three days later, after swinging in a long circuit, Conn Conagher found a job.

Seaborn Tay was forty years old when he decided to make his stand. He rode into the country alone, scouted a piece of country he liked, and although everybody warned him it was Apache country and he wouldn't last a month, he moved in, built an outfit, and by the time Conn Conagher rode up to the bunk house rustling a job, Tay had been running cattle on that range four years and he still had his hair.

Conagher swung down from his horse and looked across the yard at the man who stood on the steps.

"You ridin' the grub line, or huntin' a job?"

"A job if I can get it. A meal if I can't."

"Have you got sand?" Tay came walking down toward him. "I'll have nobody riding for me who is going to run for town the first time he sees a pony track."

Conagher took off the sheepskin coat. "Nice coat, ain't it? Warm, too. Well, I just swapped for it. I swapped two rifles I taken off two dead Apaches. The third one got off, but he was packin' lead. Does that answer your question?"

"Supper will be on the table in about half an hour. You got time to wash up and stow your gear. On this job I furnish the horses and the ammunition. I'll have no fighting among my crew. Any time you can't stand up to the work I'll give you two days' grub and a head start."

Conagher stripped his rigging from the dun and turned it into the corral, then he packed his blanket roll and Winchester to the bunk house.

It was like every other bunk house. Maybe it was a little stronger and tighter than most southern bunk houses, more like they had in Montana or Colorado. He chose an empty bunk near the stove, and threw his gear into it.

There were three hands on the job. He made a fourth. There were bunks for twelve, but only those near the stove were occupied. He checked the fire, added a couple of sticks, and unrolled his bed. He took his spare six-shooter and tucked it under his blanket, then sat down and cleaned his rifle.

By the time he had finished he heard the triangle ringing for supper, and when he went out one of the hands was just riding in. It was Kris Mahler.

"Look what the cat dragged in," Mahler said. "Did the Old Man hire you?"

"Somebody has to do the work," Conagher said. "Now I can see why he was so anxious to get a good man."

Mahler stepped down from the saddle and commenced building a smoke. "Anything strike you peculiar about this setup?"

"What's peculiar?"

"Hirin' men this time of year. Usually the old hands stay on for the winter months. Why should Tay be hirin' so late in the season? What happened to his regular hands?"

"Don't get a burr under your saddle. You'll find out soon enough. Where's the others?"

"Riding the line. It's a long two-day trip. One goes north and one south, and they swing around and pass each other. There are two line cabins, and if you time it right you can sleep inside. Mainly it's to keep stock from drifting, checking range and water holes, and keeping your eyes open for rustlers."

They walked up to the ranch house together.

"The grub's good," Mahler said. "You never ate such grub. The Old Man found him a chef who got throwed out of some ho-tel back east."

There were just four of them at the table, and the food *was* good. Conn ate a second helping, then filled his cup again and leaned back.

He talked little, listened a lot. Mahler had always been a good talker, an easy-going man, and a good hand. He had a way of talking on any subject, to anyone. Conn envied him, while he listened.

There was one old hand, a man named Leggett who had come from southeast Texas to this place, riding as segundo to Tay, who was his own foreman. The other hand, as Conn might have guessed, was Johnny McGivern. Like himself, Mahler and McGivern had ridden in hunting a job and they had been hired.

Suddenly Tay turned to Conagher. "Mahler will be telling you, anyway, so you might as well know. Two of my hands up and quit just before Mahler and McGivern rode in, and another one's missing."

"Missing?"

"Martinez. He came from Texas with me, too. He rode out, taking the south swing. Mahler saw him over east of here the next day. They talked, smoked a cigarette, and rode on. Nobody has seen Martinez since."

"A lot of things can happen," Conagher said. "This here's a rough country."

Kris Mahler tilted back in his chair and sipped coffee.

The thought came to Conagher suddenly, and he voiced it without thinking. "Do you share any range with Ladder Five?"

Mahler looked up sharply, then glanced at Tay. The rancher pushed back slightly from the table and studied Conn carefully. "What do you know about Ladder Five?"

"Well, I saw a couple of their hands over to Horse Springs. They had pretty good outfits, the both of them. I'd say they were gents who could use a brand just like they've got."

"We've had no trouble with them," Tay said. "We've no reason to expect trouble."

Conagher shrugged. "Well, I never saw them before and never expect to again. I just came here hunting a riding job."

Later, when they were outside, Mahler commented, "I wouldn't say any more about the Five, if I was you. No need letting the Old Man get the wind up."

"None of my affair," Conagher said. "I wanted a place to sit out the winter, and as long as nobody bothers me, I'll bother nobody."

And then Mahler said the wrong thing. "A man out there on a horse . . . he's all alone. He's a settin' duck for any man with a rifle. A man would be foolish to risk that now, wouldn't he?"

Conn Conagher, who never liked being pushed, felt his old cantankerous mood coming on. He'd be damned if he was going to ride scared for anybody . . . any time. But he said nothing. This, he decided, was a time to listen.

The following day Leggett rode in.

He was a tall man with a long face and a dry-as-dust

manner, but Conn pegged him right away as an honest man, as well as no fool.

Conn listened to him discuss conditions on the range, where he had seen cattle, where the water holes were, what steers were trouble makers.

Conn saddled up and tightened the cinch. He got out his Winchester and slid it into the scabbard. "You won't need that," Mahler said. "We ain't seen an Injun around in some time."

"I feel better with it," Conn replied.

Seaborn Tay walked out on the porch and called to him. "First time out," he said, "you just get acquainted with the country." Briefly he explained the layout of the range claimed by the ST, and then he added, in a somewhat lower voice, "I got nothing but respect for an honest cowhand."

Conn Conagher stepped into the saddle and gathered his reins. "Mr. Tay," he said, "I've covered a lot of country in my time, but when I take a man's money I ride for the brand."

7

Conagher covered four miles in his first hour. The range lay below six thousand feet at this point, with much open country. There were cottonwoods along the stream beds, with scrub oak, piñon, juniper, and occasional mountain mahogany on the slopes.

The range condition was fair to middling. He saw a few head of steers and several cows, all wearing the ST brand. Where they were too close to what Tay considered his line, Conagher turned them back, then rode on.

The stock was in good shape for cold weather, and there was sufficient range for the number of cattle he saw. On this first trip he was only going to get a rough idea of the country and the problems, but already he had seen a few areas where larkspur and horse bush were plentiful . . . a good idea would be to move all stock out of this area, come spring. Cattle wouldn't eat most poisonous plants if there was other forage. The trouble was that many dangerous plants were the first things to turn green in the spring. He took out his tally book and made a note of the area and its probable limits.

Just before noon he turned up a slope, found a trickle of water coming down through a grove of alders, and stepped down from the saddle. He loosened the cinch, let his horse have a little water, then picketed it on a pocket of grass and settled down to chewing on a piece of jerky.

From where he sat he could see over a far stretch of country. Getting his field glasses from his saddlebag, he began to study the country. He spotted several bunches of cattle, a few scattered ones, and a bunch of deer. He was getting up to return the field glasses to the saddlebag, but took one longer look. Further out, beyond the limits of ST range, he saw another bunch of cattle.

He studied them for a while, curious as to why they were bunched so tightly . . . and then he picked up a plume of dust and saw the cattle were being drifted by two riders. They were too far away to make them out clearly.

He tightened the cinch, swung into the saddle, and angled down the mountainside.

This was open range country, and the limits that Tay placed on his range were purely arbitrary. Such limits were probably not recognized by other ranchers; it was simply that Tay wished to keep his own herds within those limits. That way it was easier to supervise and care for them, to check range conditions, and to treat them for screw worms, and for cuts or scrapes from horns or rocks.

Conagher found the tracks of scattered cattle on Tay range, and found where they had been bunched and drifted. The tracks showed the men had ridden carelessly, as if driving the cattle by chance.

He followed the tracks, keeping to low ground and what cover he could find, until, topping out on a piñon-crested ridge, he saw the cattle not far off, still moving northward. The two riders were going on.

Holding to the cover of the piñons, Conagher considered. The cattle below were likely to be ST stock, but without checking the brands, he would not be sure. They had been started north, and would probably, unless stopped, continue to graze in that direction. With a little nudge from riders, they might be thirty miles away by the time another man came this way.

With his glasses he studied the direction taken by the two riders, but they were not in sight now. Waiting only a few minutes longer, he rode down to the herd.

All but one wore the ST brand. He cut out the lone steer, then started the others back toward their home range. He had almost reached the home range when another rider, this one on a sorrel horse with three white stockings, came down off the slope.

He was a stocky, hard-faced man with a scar over one eye, high cheekbones, and a square jaw. He was riding a Ladder Five horse.

"Where you takin' them steers?" he asked.

"Back to their home range. As you can see, they're ST stock. Figured I'd best start 'em back where they come from."

The man studied the brands, then looked at Conagher. "I don't believe I know you," he said. "Are you a new rider for Tay?"

"Uh-huh. My name's Conagher. First time around. Sort of gettin' acquainted with the range."

"I'm Tile Coker. You'd better have a talk with Kris Mahler."

"We've talked before. Kris an' me rode together for the stage company a while back."

Tile Coker gave him a quick glance. "Oh? Are you the gent who busted up Kiowa Staples?"

"We had a difficulty."

"Heard about it." Coker swung his horse. "You an' Kris should get better acquainted. Save us all some trouble."

"Maybe."

Coker rode off, and Conagher pushed the cattle back over the line and deep into ST territory. Only then did he resume his ride.

Twice he found bunches of ST cattle that seemed to have strayed too far north. He started them south, then pushed on, but he kept off the skyline and carried his Winchester in his hands.

Johnny McGivern was waiting for him near a clump of scrub oak, but Conagher saw him before he was seen by McGivern and chose to make a sweep around some brush up the slope from where Johnny waited.

McGivern saw him then and yelled, but Conagher took a slow, lazy turn around the clump of oak, cutting for sign. There was none but that left by Johnny himself, so he rode on up to the fire.

Johnny had coffee ready, and Conagher swung down.

This was apparently a place where frequent stops had been made. There were many tracks, but none of them were fresh except those made by Johnny's pinto gelding.

"The stock seems to be in good shape," Conagher said. "Some of it is drifting, though."

"Yeah?" Johnny glanced at him. "You see anybody?"

"Only a puncher named Coker. Rides for the Ladder Five."

"You talk much?"

Conagher took his cup from his saddlebag and filled it from the coffeepot. "Not much."

Johnny was looking at him, but Conagher paid no attention. He sipped the coffee gratefully. "Good coffee," he said.

"We leave the pot hanging to that cedar. Whoever gets here first, makes it."

"I'll try to see you get here before I do. You make better coffee."

"Ma taught me. Sometimes I made it for her before she got home." Johnny looked around at him. "Ma worked out. My pa was killed in a train crash when I was six."

"She had nerve," Conagher said. "It takes nerve to bring up a boy when a woman's alone." He looked over at Johnny. "She'd be proud of you, I think. You shape up like quite a man."

McGivern flushed, and to change the subject he said, "I always wished I could have known what pa was like. What kind of a man he was."

"Most railroaders I've known were mighty good men," Conagher said. "I've helped lay track, myself. And I've ridden the cars a good bit, with shipments of stock, and the like. They're good men."

"I never had a chance to know him."

"A boy should know his pa—he needs somebody

to look up to. A boy or a girl, they learn how to be a man or a woman by watching their folks."

"There was a man worked at a store near us. Sometimes when we hadn't any money he let us have groceries anyway . . . until we could pay. I don't know if ma ever did manage to pay him all of it."

"Some day you ought to go back and ask him. Pay him what you owe."

Johnny stared into his cup. "I've thought about it. You think I should?"

"Uh-huh."

They sat silent, drinking coffee and listening to the pleasant sound of the horses cropping grass. After a while, Conagher got to his feet and cinched up.

"Conn?" Johnny said questioningly.

"Yeah?"

"Why didn't you draw on that man? On Kiowa?"

"You mean was I afraid? No, I wasn't . . . not that I recollect. I expect all men are scared sometimes, but I didn't think of it. Kiowa wasn't really mean—he just had a blown-up idea of who he was . . . why should I kill him because he was making a fool of himself? Why should I risk getting killed myself, for the same reason?

"He had to be taught," Conn went on, "and there's no other way, sometimes. If he lives, he'll be grateful. If he doesn't, it won't make any difference. First thing you want to remember, boy, is that a reputation doesn't make a man tough. You got to know, not did he kill somebody, but who were they? How tough were they? Also, could he have done otherwise? A man who kills when he can do otherwise is crazy . . . plumb crazy."

"He might have killed you."

"Might have." Conagher stepped into the saddle and

looked down at Johnny McGivern. "Some men take a sight of killing, boy. Just be sure that when killing time comes around that you're standing on the right side."

Johnny stared after him. Now what did he mean by that? Did he mean anything by it?

In spite of himself, Johnny felt drawn to the strange, lonely rider who was just disappearing down a draw. He had never seen a man more alone, nor a man more secure in himself. That was it, Johnny surmised: Conn Conagher knew what he believed . . . and Johnny wished he did himself.

Kris now . . . Kris had swagger and style, but something about Kris made Johnny uneasy.

But only since he had met Conn Conagher.

That was the day Conn found the first of the notes. He saw it from far off, and drew up in the shadow of a juniper to study it out.

Down there on the flat there was a speck of white, just a speck, but it had no business to be there.

Conagher had been less than fourteen when he learned to distrust something out of place, and what he saw was not sunlight on a stone, it was not the bottom side of a leaf; it looked like a bit of paper.

It was not much over a hundred yards off, so he put his glass on it.

A piece of paper lying amongst some tumbleweed. His glasses swept the ground . . . no tracks that he could see at this distance.

Warily, he rode along, scouting the area until he was sure there was no one around. Then he rode up to the tumbleweed.

The paper was folded over several times and it was tied to the tumbleweed. Curious, he untied it and opened the paper.

Sometimes when I am alone I feel
I will die if I do not talk to someone, and
I am alone so much.
I love to hear the wind in the grass,
or in the cedars.

He read it through, then read it again. He started to throw it aside, but then he tucked it into his vest pocket.

He liked the wind in the grass, himself. And the cedars, too, and the smell of them. He wondered if the writer of that note had ever really looked at a cedar. Gnarled, twisted by wind, rooted often enough in rock, still it lived and grew. It took a sight of living and hardship to grow like that, but when they did grow they grew strong, and they lasted. Why, he'd seen cedars that had split rocks apart, cedars that must have been old before Columbus landed.

Leggett was sitting in front of the bunk house when Conagher rode in. The old man looked up. "We've et," he said, "but coffee's on. The Old Man figured you might come in late."

"Thanks."

Conagher stripped the rigging from his horse and threw it over a saddle tree under the shed. He was dog-tired and bone-weary.

"McGivern come in?"

"Nope . . . Kris took off some place, too."

Conagher dumped water into the washbasin beside the door and, rolling up his sleeves, he took off his hat and neckerchief and washed his face, neck, and arms. Then he dried them on the roller towel, hitched his gunbelt into place, and started for the house.

Then he stopped. "Leggett, you might as well have some coffee with me. You'll grow right into that bench if you set there much longer."

Leggett got up and walked along with him to the patch of light that fell from the kitchen door.

"The Old Man's turned in, but he said you'd better pick yourself a couple of good winter horses and iron them out a little, to suit you."

"All right."

"Tay's got good stock. There's a big dapple-gray would make quite a horse if you're man enough to take the kinks out of him, and there's a buckskin about the same size. Both of them big enough and strong enough for the snow."

"Does she get deep around here?"

"In the draws and canyons she piles up. You'll need Montana-style horses."

They sat in silence for a time, and then Conagher refilled his cup. "You been on this range quite a while. How's the Old Man when it comes to trouble?"

Leggett gave Conagher a bleak look. "He'll stand by you, if that's what you mean, but nobody else will. I'm the only one of the old hands left, and I'm only here because I ain't a youngster no more and I got nowhere to go."

Leggett got to his feet. "I don't know you, cowboy, an' you don't know me. If you got any ideas about buckin' trouble you got to go it alone."

"You won't help me?"

"How much help would I be? I'm up in my sixties, boy, older than you thought, an' I want to live out my days, not die on some sandy slope with lead in my guts."

"And the Old Man?"

Leggett looked at him. "Ain't that what they want most? If they can get him out on the range they'll kill him, and then they can take the cattle as they want, and nobody to stop them."

Conn Conagher was a stubborn man. He had never

given much thought to truth and justice or the rights of man, but he did not like what seemed to be happening here, and anything that happened to an outfit he rode for, happened to him.

"Will you stand by the Old Man?" he asked. "Supposin' they come after him?"

"I'll fight. If they come after him, I'll fight."

"All right, then you stay here. You keep a rifle handy, and if there's any doubt—shoot."

8

Kris Mahler rode in about an hour later. Conn was seated in the bunk house with his feet up on a box reading a dog-eared copy of a magazine. He knew by the way Mahler stalked into the room that the man was angry.

"Conn, what's got into you? We've got a good thing here if you play your cards right."

"I play them the way they're dealt, Kris. What don't you like?"

"There's no need to stir up trouble. You wanted a place to lay up during the winter . . . well, you got it. So set still and ride it out. In the spring you can drift."

Conagher glanced around. "When I take a man's money, Kris, I do the job he hired me for. I don't know no other way."

"No, I guess you don't." Mahler dropped onto a bench. "Conn, you're no tenderfoot. The Ladder Five is Smoke Parnell's outfit. Tile Coker is his right hand.

You run a-foul of them and they'll nail your hide to the barn door."

Slowly, Conagher lowered his feet. Every time somebody warned him or threatened him it got his back up. He wanted trouble with no man, but he wasn't going to take any pushing around, either.

"You tell me something, Mahler. Where do you stand? Are you riding for the brand? Are you runnin' scared? Or are you sellin' out to that damned bunch of highbinders on the Ladder?"

Mahler's face turned ugly. "I could make you draw a gun for that," he said hoarsely. "Damn you, Conn! Don't push me!"

"Seems to me," Conagher replied mildly, "that I am the one who is being pushed. I'll tell you this, Mahler, and put it in your pipe and smoke it. Every ST beef critter I see heading toward Ladder range is going to get turned back, and if I smell any hide burning from a Ladder iron, I'll go in a-fogging it . . . no matter who is doing the branding. Do you hear me?"

"You're a damn fool," Mahler said. "Look, they're going to clean him out. By spring there won't be a head of beef left on ST range, and there isn't a thing anybody can do about it. You can do your job an' look the other way, or you can set yourself up for a target. You've got a choice."

"It's you who have the choice, Mahler. You've got the choice right this minute. You throw your pack on your horse and ride out of here tonight, or you do what you mentioned, and pull that gun on me.

"Before you reach for it, remember this. I been shot at a few times, and I'm still around. I've gone down a few times, but I always got some lead into the man who did the shooting."

Conn Conagher stood up. "Kris, you pack up and light a shuck. I got no use for a traitor."

Mahler got to his feet, his features dark with fury. Desperately, he wanted to pull a gun on Conagher, but there was a healthy streak of caution in him.

There was nothing of the tenderfoot in Conagher. He was an old curly wolf from the high country, and Mahler had seen what he did to Staples. That beating had been brutal and thorough. Moreover, in the close confines of a bunk house there was no way either of them could miss. Kris Mahler was ready enough to shoot, but he was not ready to die.

"All right," he said, "I'll pull out. And Johnny will go with me. That means there's just you, the Old Man, and Leggett . . . how far will that take you?"

Conagher shrugged. "Kris, neither of us is going to get out of this alive. That's the only thing a man knows about life.

"I'll work my tail off and cash in my chips some dark night riding herd on another man's cows, but when they write my epitaph they'll say, *He rode for the brand,* and when they write yours they'll say, *He sold out the man who trusted him.* I like mine better."

"You're a damn fool," Mahler said.

"Am I? I've seen your kind, Kris. Whatever you steal, the women on the Line will get, or you'll get headaches from the rotten booze they feed you, and when your back is turned one of your partners will shoot you for what's left in your pockets."

Kris Mahler walked to the door, dropped his gear, and went to saddle a horse.

Seaborn Tay came to the door of the ranch house. "Kris? Is that you?" he called.

"He's just quit, Mr. Tay," Conn said. "He's workin' for the Ladder outfit now."

"You got money coming, Mahler," Tay said.

"He's got nothing coming. He's helping them rob you."

"Nevertheless, I am paying him. Come to the house, Mahler, when you're ready to go."

"There's a square man, Kris," Conagher said.

Mahler did not speak, but when his horse was saddled he turned on Conagher. "Tell him to keep his damn money! I don't want it!"

"Better take it. That may be the last honest money you ever see."

Mahler turned around sharply. "Lay off, Conagher. Damn you, lay off! I don't want to kill you, but—"

"Arizona is nice this time of year, if you go south far enough," Conn suggested, "or California, or the gulf coast of Texas."

Suddenly a rider came in from the dark. It was Johnny McGivern.

He looked startled when he saw Mahler packing his gear behind the saddle. "Hey, what's goin' on here?"

"I just quit, kid. Get your outfit and let's go."

"Go where?"

"I'm joining up with the Ladder Five. Come on. I ain't got all night."

Johnny stared at him, then looked at Conagher. "Is this your doing?"

"No, his. He decided he didn't want to swindle a man who paid him honest wages. He's going where he belongs, of his own choice."

"You talk too damn much!" Mahler said. "Come on, kid."

"There it lays, Johnny. You've got a choice. You can ride the owl-hoot trail, or you can play it honest. What you decide tonight can change your whole life."

"Kris is my partner!"

"Right down the road to hell, or to a hangman's noose. That the way you want it?"

"Lay off, Conn!" Mahler exclaimed. "I'm warnin' you. *Lay off!*"

"Can't you see it, Mahler? I'm never going to lay off. I'm going to show those friends of yours what it costs to steal an honest man's cattle. From the moment you ride out of here, it's war, Kris, and I don't have one ounce of mercy in me for your kind."

"You're only one man."

"I know. And there was a Texas ranger named Captain Bill MacDonald who said there was no stoppin' a man who knew he was in the right and kept a-comin'.

"You boys had better shoot me, Kris, and then you'd better shoot me again and stomp the life out of me, because as long as I can crawl, I'll fight. As long as I can move a finger, I'll squeeze a trigger. You boys have saddled your bronc, now let's see if you can ride him!"

"Johnny, you goin' to stand there? Come on!"

"Conn? What'll I do?"

"You're a man, son," Conagher answered. "You make your own decision. Just remember when you make this bet you've thrown your life into the pot . . . your life and your future."

Johnny hesitated, then slowly he got down from the saddle. "I'll stay. You ride on, Kris. I'm sorry, but this here's where the trail divides."

"The hell with you!"

Kris Mahler jerked his horse around savagely and rode out of the yard.

Conagher looked at the boy. There were tears in his eyes. Conn put a hand on his shoulder. "Come on, son. You need something to eat."

The next morning, leaving Johnny McGivern on the ranch, Conn Conagher took off, but instead of making the wide sweep he rode directly across country. From the top of a ridge he studied the layout with his field glasses for nearly half an hour before he rode down to the flat.

Then he began a sweep, pushing cattle back toward the canyons of the Black Range where there was water and grass, as well as some shelter from the weather. He worked hard, starting several bunches moving, and stopping every once in a while to study the range to the north.

Then he rode on, keeping under cover, starting cattle whenever he encountered them, having the one idea of getting them as deep into ST territory as possible.

It was late afternoon before he saw any riders, and when he did see them he turned at once toward the hills, riding back toward the ridge by a route he had previously scouted. Leaving his horse out of sight beyond the ridge, he dug out a small hollow in a place that seemed to offer no cover, and there he watched the riders. One of them was young, the second was, by the look of him, Smoke Parnell himself.

Suddenly they drew up. Conagher swore. They had found his tracks!

He eased his rifle forward and waited, watching to see what they would do.

Parnell studied the tracks, then scanned the country around, particularly the ridge where Conagher lay, but farther to the east and west in places of obvious cover. Then he reached for his rifle, and when he put a hand on it, Conagher tucked the butt of his own rifle against his shoulder, his cheek against the stock, and took a good sight. He squeezed off his shot as Parnell's rifle began to leave the scabbard.

He saw the horse jump and go to pitching even as the boom of the shot reverberated against the hills. Instantly Conn was on his feet and running for his horse.

When he reached the crest of the ridge again, fifty yards off, he was in the saddle, and only his eyes cleared the ridge, behind some brush.

Parnell was getting up off the ground, and he was

shouting mad. His horse had run off a few steps, and the rider with Parnell had gone after it. Parnell stooped to pick up his rifle and Conagher shot again, his bullet kicking sand within inches of Parnell's hand.

The outlaw leaped back so swiftly that he tripped himself and fell again. Instantly, Conn fired again, splashing sand into Parnell's face; then switching his aim, he put a bullet in front of the horse just as the other rider was reaching for the bridle. The frightened horse, evidently burned by the first bullet as it ricocheted, now took off running.

The rider wheeled his horse and rode back, lending a stirrup to Parnell. Just as Parnell lifted a foot to the stirrup, Conagher coolly shot again, kicking sand under the horse's belly.

The horse lunged, and Parnell, his foot caught in the stirrup, fell to the sand, and the plunging horse dragged him twenty feet before its rider calmed the animal enough for Parnell to get up.

Conagher checked his position as he fed shells into the magazine. He had dismounted for more accurate shooting, and now he walked back and mounted up. When he let his eyes clear the ridge again, the horse carrying two riders was some distance off, and out of rifle shot.

Conagher worked on until sundown, pushing strays back toward the mountains. Once they got into those canyons where there was plenty of water and good grass it would be the devil's own job to round them up and get them out. And as he knew, outlaws have no particular drive toward hard work.

It was long after dusk when he started back, and midnight before he finally rode into the ranch yard.

There was a movement in the shadows near the house, and Seaborn Tay walked out into the open.

"Worried about you, boy. Your horse looks beat, plumb beat."

Conagher dismounted, stripped the rigging from his horse, and roped another. As he did so, he explained, and added, "Might as well let them know it isn't all going to be fun," he said. "Might be they'll lose their taste for it."

"Not them," Tay said. "Not Smoke Parnell."

"They've been warned. Now they'll come a-hunting blood. You got to be ready for them." Conagher walked into the kitchen and dropped wearily into a chair. "I'm going out on the trail . . . bed down and wait for them."

He ate slowly, relishing every bite, scarcely aware that he had eaten nothing in many hours. But he could feel the heaviness in his muscles. He needed sleep—needed it the worst way, but he had started something today that would take some time to quiet down.

"We need men," Tay said. "You can't carry this on by yourself. Leggett's old, and McGivern . . . well, he'll get himself killed. He'll try too hard, I'm thinking."

"Leave it to me. You hold the place, I'll move around and make it kind of unpleasant for them."

Suddenly his eyes brightened. "I've got an idea where we might find a man. It's a gamble, but worth the chance."

When he left the house he went out and shook Johnny awake. "How'd you like to ride, fifty, sixty miles?"

"Where?"

Sitting down on a bench, Conagher traced out the route. "Now you hold to it. Don't try no short cuts, because there ain't any in that country. Keep a sharp watch out for Indians . . . maybe they'll be there, maybe they won't. The man we want is trappin' back yonder—his name is Chip Euston. I don't have any idea whether he'll come, but if he does come he'll be worth any three of those outlaws."

When Johnny McGivern rode off, taking a route that would avoid towns, Conn rode out on the trail down which he expected the Ladder Five to come. When he got out a way, he rode off the trail, climbed a ridge, and bedded down where he could look around him and listen.

He was trusting more to his horse than to himself. He had deliberately chosen a mountain-bred mustang, a horse only a few months away from running wild. He wanted a horse that was spooky . . . that would hear every sound . . . and a horse could both see and hear better than a man.

He slept fitfully, awakening to listen and look, dozing off again. At daylight the country was empty as far as his eyes could reach. A slow smoke lifted from the chimney at the ranch, and wearily he climbed into the saddle and rode back.

"They didn't come," Tay said.

"No, but they will. They will."

He went to the bunk house and tumbled into his bunk and slept.

Tay and Leggett could keep watch. He would sleep.

9

For some time after he awoke he lay still, staring up at the bottom of the bunk above him. The room was shadowed and still, and he heard no sound outside. He was still tired, but he had often been tired, and simply being so did not offer a reason for lying abed.

But he was more than tired. And perhaps because he was tired he was feeling again that dreadful, depressing loneliness that came to him sometimes.

Was it that which led him to fight for the brand for which he rode? Was it actually because he was an honest man, or was it simply that he clung to the brand, the outfit for which he rode, as the one stable thing in his transient world?

He was not, he told himself, gifted with much imagination. He simply did what had to be done, and his code of ethics was the code of his father, his family, and his time. It would be easy, he told himself, to throw everything overboard and disclaim any responsibility. All he had to do was saddle up and ride out of the country.

It sounded easy, but it was not that easy, even if a man could leave behind his sense of guilt at having deserted a cause. To be a man was to be responsible. It was as simple as that. To be a man was to build something, to try to make the world about him a bit easier to live in for himself and those who followed.

You could sneer at that, you could scoff, you could refuse to acknowledge it, but when it came right down to it, Conn decided it was the man who planted a tree, dug a well, or graded a road who mattered.

He was a loner—he had always been a loner. He was as covered with spines as any porcupine. He was cantankerous and edgy. Outwardly easy-going, he shied away from people, wary of the traps surrounding people that could lead to trouble. Yet once in trouble, he knew of no other way than to fight it out to a finish.

Conagher had worked too hard too many times to like a thief or a vandal who would steal or destroy the efforts of other men. Maybe in the last analysis what they said of him was true, that he didn't give a damn —about himself or those who got in his way. He did have a few principles, and he had not thought much about them. They were few, they were simple, they were his. And he lived by them.

He swung his feet to the floor and fumbled for his socks. He would have to stay put long enough to do some laundry, he decided, looking at a sock. He pulled it on, and then the other, tugged on his boots, and stamped into them.

He reached for his gunbelt, slung it about his hips, and went to the door.

The bullet struck the door jamb, scattering splinters, and he jerked back so sharply he almost fell. Wheeling around, he ran for his Winchester.

The door was standing open now, but there was no other sound from outside. He glanced at the place where the bullet had hit, and then from well back in the room he knelt down and followed its probable trajectory to a low hill a good four hundred yards away. Back in the shadows of the interior of the bunk house, he studied that hill. Then he moved farther back to the second window, which was well toward the back of the building. As he thought, the view from that window was obscured by the corner posts of the corral and its watering trough.

There was no sound from the house. The horses were quiet in the corral. Moving around, he studied the view from the two windows on the opposite side of the bunk house.

Was this an all-out attack? Or was it the work of one disgruntled enemy?

Where was Johnny McGivern? Where were the Old Man and Leggett? Then he remembered: he had sent McGivern into the mountains to recruit Chip Euston if possible.

The windows on the far side of the bunk house looked toward the stable and to the open range beyond, but

Conn distrusted what he saw. That plain out there looked too level and innocent; there could be dips and hollows that could hide the body of a man. He had a hunch that was the idea: first, the shot from the other side, then he was to try to get out on the far side, and when well out of the window he would be killed.

He moved restlessly from window to window. That man out there on the grass, if there was one, had better be a good Indian, because he was going to have to wait ... and wait.

Conagher liked the look of the corral post and the trough. It was the best cover, but for the time being he would simply watch and wait.

Nothing moved out there. The bunk house was strongly built and could stand a long attack if necessary. As yet he had not fired a shot, and they might believe he was dead. They had shot as he started to leave the door, and he had fallen back out of sight. If they did believe it they would soon come to investigate.

The floor of the bunk house was puncheon and did not squeak, so they could not hear any movements within. A slow half-hour passed. He poured a cup of coffee from the pot that sat on the stove. It was strong and scalding, but it tasted good.

He was in no hurry. Conn Conagher had lived through too many range wars, too many Indian troubles to hurry. He knew how those men felt out there in the open. They had taken up their positions before daylight, and they had now been waiting three hours or more. During all that time they had had a chance to fire only once.

The night had been cold, but the chill was leaving the air now, and it would be getting warm out there. No doubt they had water, but he had shelter, coffee, and plenty of ammunition. Let 'em wait.

Nevertheless, he went from window to window, always remaining well back in the room where there was less chance of being seen. There was a limit to patience, unless you were an Indian, or Conn Conagher.

Suddenly he saw movement, or rather the shadow of movement beyond the corral. Somebody had crept along the ground close to the corral on the opposite side, and was nearing a post at the corner identical with the one Conn had planned to use for cover. From the window where he now watched he could not see the crawler, but he could see tiny puffs of dust from his movements. There was a chance that when he reached the end of the corral, with the protection of the post and the buttressing posts that strengthened the corners, he would rise to a standing position. And when he did he would show a portion of his body between the poles of the corral.

Conagher took a quick run around the windows, glancing out, and then came back. Again he saw a tiny puff of dust. He eased the window up, and it made no sound. Carefully, he took aim at the opening that seemed to offer the best chance. He took up the slack on the trigger, set his sight picture on a point of the gap nearest the post, and waited.

Perspiration trickled down his cheek, down his neck. The morning had grown warmer and he was close to the stove. He held his slack and continued to wait.

Suddenly a spot of blue showed where he held his aim, and he squeezed off his shot.

He heard the thud of the bullet, for the man was no more than sixty feet away. The thud sounded so loud that for a moment he believed he had hit one of the poles, but then he heard the clatter of a rifle against the poles as it fell, and the moan of a man who has been hard hit.

It was the first shot he had fired, and only the second shot fired since the attack began.

There were no answering shots, and there was no movement. For several minutes he waited, moving from window to window, expecting an attack now . . . or would they still wait, perhaps until dark?

Suddenly he heard a shuddering groan from the man beyond the corral.

"You hit bad?" he asked, hoping his voice would carry no further than the wounded man.

"Yes, damn you!"

"Well, you came askin' for it. I didn't put out no invitations."

There was no reply, and after a bit he said, "If you want to call your friends, I'll let 'em come get you, but the first one who lifts a gun gets killed."

"They won't believe you."

"That's your problem. I'll see no man suffer, and whoever you are, I'd advise you if you live through this to get yourself some new friends . . . if they don't come after you."

"I can't . . . I couldn't make 'em hear."

The injured man's voice sounded weak, and Conagher moved to the door and called out: "You got a hurt man down here. If you want to come get him, leave your rifles behind and come on. I'll kill the first man who tries a shot."

There was a long silence, then all of a sudden a voice rang out, "Hold your fire! I'm coming down!"

The man stood up, half crouching as if ready to fall back, but when there was no shot he came on, slowly at first. He was young, curly-haired . . . Conagher had heard of him. Scott, his name was, a new recruit.

"He ain't turned sour yet," Conagher said. "There's a chance for him."

He spoke to himself, but he said it loud enough for the wounded man to hear, if he was conscious. Conagher's shot probably had gone through his body side to side, but that was only a guess. When he had fired he thought he saw the tips of the cartridges in the man's belt just under his aiming point, but he could not be sure.

Scott was coming on down the slope. He had slowed some more, but he was walking along.

"The boy's got sand," Conagher said, speaking aloud again, "and he's got some show-off in him, too. He's taking this like a big Injun."

Scott had reached the wounded man now, and he stood up straight. "You inside! I can't carry this man! He'd die before we'd gone any distance. He's gut-shot, and bad."

Was it a trick? Conagher wasn't worried about tricks. Those that he hadn't used himself had been used on him. "All right, kid, bring him on inside."

"You want me to drop my gunbelt?"

"You keep your gun. And if you feel lucky, grab for it. I'll not kill any man who isn't packing iron."

Scott picked up the wounded man and carried him to the bunk-house door, brought him inside, and put him down gently on a bunk.

The wounded man was Hi Jackson, one of the two men Conagher had encountered at Horse Spring station. Blood soaked the lower part of his shirt and the front of his pants around the belt. The bullet, as Conagher has surmised, had gone in at one side and out the other, and it was an ugly wound.

Scott's face was pale. Evidently he had not seen much blood before, and now it was on his own shirt and hands.

"You can wash up outside the door," Conagher said, "if you want to chance it."

Scott glanced at him. "You must be Conagher. You don't think much of us, do you?"

"A bunch of damn two-bit thieves that would rustle

an old man's cows? No, I don't think much of you. If Smoke Parnell had the guts of a mouse he'd get out and earn himself a living instead of robbing old men."

The boy flushed, and Conagher studied him coldly. "No, kid, if you want to know, I don't see anything a damn bit exciting about what you're doin' now. I don't think it takes nerve, and I don't think it's romantic, like some folks seem to think. The outfit you're tied up with are a bunch of dry-gulchin' thieves."

Scott turned to go. "You better do some thinkin', boy," Conagher said. "You look like you had the makings, and it took sand to come down here after this man. Look at your hole card, kid, and quit this bunch."

"They're my friends."

"They were his friends, too. They knowed him a lot longer than you have, but who came after him? And who'd come after you? Kid, it's just pure luck that you're standin' here talkin' with me instead of lyin' on that bunk, gut-shot."

"Can you do anything for him?"

"Why the hell should I? He was comin' after me when he got it. But I will, kid, I will because I'm a damn fool, if I can find the time while I'm standin' off your friends."

Conagher moved back, watching the windows. "Your friends are waitin' until dark when the lot of them can come down here and jump me. Well, I've got some money here, boy, and I'll bet you the stack that I take at least two more, and likely three, and you can be one of them."

Scott stood still, his face still pale, anger fighting with indecision. "You can stay here if you like," Conagher said, "and mind your friend, if friend he is."

"You'd trust me?"

"Not a damn bit. If you made a wrong move I'd shoot you dead in your tracks. But you're better off down here than out there. You got a chance, kid. You'd better take it."

"I . . . I can't. I'd be a traitor. I'd be—"

"A traitor to them? All right, boy, you've had your say, now get out and get on back up the hill, but when you come down again, you better be using that gun, because I'm going to be aiming for your guts."

"You're a hard man, Conagher."

"This here's a hard country. But it's a good country, Scott, and it'll be better as soon as we hang or shoot a few more thieving skunks."

His face white to the lips, Scott went out. He hesitated, then started the long walk up the hill. Conagher watched him go, knowing how long and hard a walk the the boy was taking. He was going back to his outlaw companions, when deep down inside he knew he shouldn't. He was going back out of misplaced loyalty.

Suddenly Conagher shouted, "Scott, you tell Smoke Parnell that if he has the guts of a jack rabbit he'll come down here and we'll shoot it out, man to man. He's supposed to be gun-handy. Me, I'm just a cow puncher."

When Scott got over the crest, Pete Casuse, Tile Coker, and Smoke Parnell were waiting for him. "Took you long enough," Smoke said. "What happened to Hi?"

"He's been shot in the belly. It's pretty bad, I guess."

"Tough, but while Conagher's carin' for him he ain't watchin' for us?"

Curly Scott looked at him, then repeated what Conagher had said.

"I heard him," Parnell said carelessly, "an' why should I be a fool? We got him right where we want him, and come dark we'll go in after him."

Curly Scott dropped to the ground. He wished he

was anywhere but here. He had seen that man down there. He was unshaven and down at heel, he was no kid, and he was alone, but there was something about him . . .

"That's a tough man down there," he said quietly, "and we still don't know where Leggett and Tay are."

"Hell, they've quit! They taken out durin' the night. That damn fool down there is fighting for a brand that's quit him."

Conn Conagher, with occasional glances from the window, cleaned up the gunshot and bandaged the man as well as he could with what was at hand.

He looked toward the house. There had been no sign of life over there. Maybe they had left him. Maybe they had pulled out while he was asleep, Well, no matter—he wasn't quitting. Maybe he was just too dumb to quit.

10

The wounded man was muttering, and suddenly he asked for water. Conn brought it to him in the long-handled drinking gourd and held it for him while he drank.

Hi Jackson looked up at him. "I'm in pretty bad shape, ain't I?"

"I'd say so."

"You're Conagher?"

"Uh-huh. . . . The kid brought you in—Scott."

"He's . . . he's a good boy. He ought to go home."

Then Jackson lay quiet, breathing heavily. He'd lost a lot of blood, and Conagher didn't think he had much time.

"I got to leave you pretty quick. When it's dark your outfit will be down here after me."

"You ain't goin' to make it, Conagher. You know that, don't you?"

"I know nothing of the kind. But if I don't make it, they will be buryin' four or five of your boys with me. They didn't pick on no pilgrim. I've been through this a time or two."

Shadows stretched out from the house, gathered in the lee of the bunk house. Now . . . soon there would be no more time.

He filled a cup with the black coffee and sipped it while making his rounds of the windows. Then he stuffed his pockets with shells, glanced again at the wounded man, and edged over to the window.

Again he looked toward the ranch house. Where were Tay and Leggett? Suddenly he glimpsed a shadow, the shadow of a running man. There was no time for a shot, no time for anything.

He went out the window and made it to the corral corner in a long, swift dive. A man moved near the far corner, and as he moved a rifle shattered the stillness and the running man fell sprawling. Instantly there were three more shots, all of them from the house!

Another man was down, and Conn could hear somebody swearing.

Whoever was in the house had wisely held their fire until the attackers expected no danger from that quarter. Two men were down now, and the one in plain sight was dead.

Crouched at the corner of the corral, Conn saw a flicker of movement—something white. He looked again, and saw that it was a paper tied to a tumbleweed—another message like the one he had found before.

It was within reach, and he put out a hand and cautiously untied it. It was too dark to read it, and he thrust it carefully down into his pocket.

The dusk was deceiving. Straining his eyes, he tried to make out some further movement, but there was none.

In another minute he heard a whisper. "Tile? Back out . . . we're pullin' away."

There was a shuffling movement of someone crawling along the ground. Conn had his gun up and could have scored a sure hit, but what was the use?

If he fired now they would surely return his fire and he would likely get hit. If they were pulling out, let them go. There was no point in it if they were quitting. Smoke Parnell had never had more than nine or ten men that Conn knew of, though there could be more . . . and he had lost three here today.

Conn stayed right where he was, and after a while he heard the drumming of hoofs, growing fainter in the distance.

By now it was completely dark, and he went back to the bunk house and stirred up the fire in the stove. Through the light from the open door he saw that Hi Jackson was dead.

He struck a match and lighted one of the lamps, keeping away from the windows in case one of the outlaws had lingered behind, though he did not expect it of them. After all, they had nothing at stake. They could ride off and attack again at another time, if they had the stomach for it.

He stood for a moment, reluctant at last to leave the bunk house. When he did, it was just as Tay and Leggett emerged from the ranch house.

"Conagher?" It was Tay speaking. "You made a fight."

"I tried."

"Most of the time we weren't situated to get in even one shot, and then we got our chance."

"You broke their backs. You took the heart out of them," Conagher said. He pushed his hat back. "I'm hungry and tired, Tay, and there's a dead man in the bunk house. The one Scott brought in."

"Who was it?"

"Hi Jackson."

"Too bad," Tay said. "He rode for me for a while. He was a good hand, but he took to riding with bad company."

"Leave him to me," Leggett said. "You done your share, Conn."

Conagher walked back to the house with Tay and sat at the table while the boss filled a cup with coffee for him, and set out bread, some cold meat, and a quarter of an apple pie.

"You must be starved," Tay said.

Conn ate without talking, and Tay stood at the window watching Leggett carry the dead man out to the hill.

"A man isn't long for this world, but he should come to something better than that. Ever think of the hereafter, Conn?"

"Not much. I figure it's like the Plains Indians say—a happy hunting ground. Leastways, that's how I'd like it to be. A place with mountains, springs, running streams, and some green, grassy banks where a man can lie with his hat over his eyes and let the bees buzz."

Somehow that made him think of the note in his pocket and he took it out and fumbled it open. He was so tired he was ready to sleep right there, half through his meal. He looked at the written words. There was just one line.

I have never been in love.

He stared at it for a long moment, then put it back in his pocket. That was a hard thing for a woman to tell herself, unless she was a youngster. What kind of a woman would write something like that and send it rolling off before the wind?

A lonely one, he told himself, a mighty lonely one.

He knew how she felt. Sometimes a body just had to have somebody to talk to. You saw something and you wanted to turn and say, *Isn't that beautiful?* And there was nobody there.

Well, there were a lot of lonely folks out here in the West. Men and women working alone, or feeling alone, their homes far from each other, their minds and hearts reaching out across the distance, plucking at the strings of the air to find some answering call.

Lonely people, who looked at horizons and wondered what, or who, was beyond them, people hemmed in by distance, people locked in space, in the emptiness . . . prisoners, they were.

In his own way Conagher was a prisoner. He'd never had the education to escape it, if that was an escape. He'd gone to work as soon as he was big enough to wrap his hands around a tool, and he'd been at it ever since. About all he'd ever had out of life was a seat in a saddle and a lot of open country to look at.

He had stifled in the dust of the drag of many a trail drive, stifled in the heat rising from two thousand hot, moving bodies. He'd had his guts churned on the seat of a stage coach bouncing over the prairie, and by many a bronc, breaking horses for the rough string.

He wished it was spring so the wind could blow back

the other way. He would like to send a message back to the one who had written these notes, to say that she was not alone, that somebody had read her words. But the wind didn't blow that way, and the chances were she'd not find it, anyway.

Tay interrupted his thoughts.

"What will they do now?" he asked. "What do you think, Conagher?"

"They won't leave us alone. Next time they'll choose a different way . . . they may just try to drive the cattle off, or take us one by one."

"Have you ever been shot, Conagher?"

"A couple of times, and it is not a rewarding experience."

He finished the pie, drank another cup of coffee, and pushed back from the table. "I'm going to sleep," he said. "Don't wake me unless there's trouble, real trouble."

He was staggering with weariness as he walked back to the bunk house. He pulled off his boots and gunbelt, simply rolled over on the bed and went to sleep. In his sleep he dreamed of whole battalions of tumbleweeds, each with its message, all blowing toward him. He grasped at each one, struggling to get its message before the wind took it out of reach.

For a week after that, there was quiet. Conagher rode to the Plaza and reported the shootings. The sheriff listened, paring his fingernails with a jackknife, and at the end of Conn's recital he got up and held out his hand.

"I know Seaborn Tay," he said. "He's a good man. A solid man. And I know Leggett. I don't know you, but I've heard about you, and I want to shake your hand. You've helped rid the country of some bad men."

He went on, "You mentioned Curly Scott. Was he hurt, do you know?"

"I doubt it."

Conagher pushed his hat back. "Sheriff, there's a boy who'd cut loose from that crowd, given the right chance. He's stuck by them through some fool sense of loyalty . . . and they don't deserve it."

"Maybe we have what it will take," the sheriff said. "His sister is in town. If you see him, tell him that. She's come from the East to see him."

And then he added, "She has no idea he's an outlaw."

When he returned from the Plaza, Conagher resumed, with the occasional help of Leggett, the slow job of moving the cattle back to more easily guarded areas. And then one day Johnny McGivern rode in.

"You didn't tell me what that country was like," Johnny said accusingly. "I lost myself two, three times."

"Did you find him?" Conagher asked.

"He's comin'. It'll take him a day or two, with what he had to do." Johnny glanced around. "From what I hear, you won't need him."

"We'll need him."

Riding alone, and riding wide over the land, Conagher found himself watching the tumbleweeds. But a week passed before he found another note, and then it was by merest chance. He had come down a draw that opened on the plain and found an old corral, built for trapping wild horses. Made of poles and brush, utilizing what was at hand, the corral had long since been abandoned, and was now breached in several places; but piled against the north wall was a mat of tumbleweeds.

He rode up to them and checked them from force of habit, and found two of the notes.

The first one, almost illegible, must have been written months ago.

When I was a little girl I dreamed
of a handsome knight who would come on a white
charger and carry me away.
        Where, O where are you, White Knight?
I have waited so long, so very long!

The second note was written much later, judging
by the freshness of the ink and the better condition of
the paper.

Last night I walked out to look up
at the stars. I wish I knew the names of the
stars.

Almost without realizing it, Conn had begun to build
an image of the girl who wrote those strange notes. She
was young, slender, and blonde, and she was somebody
he could talk to, somebody as lonely as he was himself.

"Don't fool yourself," he said aloud. "She ain't writing those notes for any leather-skinned cowpuncher like
you."

The work went on. Johnny helped with the cattle, and
they gained ground. They saw nothing of the Parnell
outfit, although Tile Coker had been to the Plaza. A
stage had been held up over in Black Canyon, some
distance to the west. None of the outlaws had been
recognized, but there had been four of them, with a
fifth holding the horses.

For a week, then, Conagher stayed around the ranch.
He repaired the corral gate, broke two horses for the
rough string, dehorned a quarrelsome steer, and cut
wood against the coming of colder weather.

Snow fell at the end of the week, just a light skim-
ming over that was gone with the first sun; but during
the next week more snow fell and the ground was

covered. The weather settled down to still, cold days and nights, and Johnny and Conn were busy breaking the ice in water holes and checking on the stock.

It was hard, bitterly cold work, and many a day Conn got down from the saddle five or six times to walk some warmth back into his feet.

Chip Euston was in the bunk house when Conagher rode back one day. The hunter looked up. "Trouble all over?"

"It'll come any day now," Conagher replied. "Keep yourself armed and ready."

Little by little Conn had taken over the ramrodding of the ranch, and nobody objected. Seaborn Tay stayed quiet, resting a lot, and Conn had a hunch the boss suffered from a bad heart.

The following morning when Conagher saddled up he planned only a short ride. However, he tied a blanket-roll behind his saddle, for a man might get caught out somewhere in this weather and he'd better be ready for a long night in the cold.

He had not gone more than four miles from headquarters when he came on the tracks of a bunch of cattle. They were bunched tightly, perhaps twenty head, and were driven by three riders on big, free-striding horses.

Making a little cairn of stones to indicate the direction taken, Conagher started north.

The trail of the cattle led straight in that direction, and the riders apparently had no worry about being discovered.

It might be a trap—it probably was. And as he thought that, a cool finger touched his cheek, another his forehead. Conn looked up . . . it was snowing. The thieves must have expected it; within an hour all trail would be wiped out.

Nevertheless, Conagher held to it. He had a couple

of frozen biscuits with him, a chunk of bacon, some jerky, and coffee. He would take his chances.

All through the morning and into the afternoon he followed the trail, which held straight north, but by mid-afternoon the trail was gone, wiped out by the snow.

He rode over into a patch of scrub oak mixed with pine, and made camp.

11

Evie Teale tied the scarf over her head as she looked out the window. The slowly falling flakes were beautiful, but they brought to her a chill of fear. The winter would be long, and it would take a good deal of fuel to heat the cabin. The pile of wood behind the cabin had grown, but judging by the past few weeks since it had grown colder, Evie knew the pile would never last through the winter.

Laban had been working steadily part of each day to build up the supply. Ruthie and Evie herself had gone far into the hills, gathering scattered fallen small branches into a pile to be dragged back to the ranch.

Charlie McCloud had come by, riding over on his own time, to help them. It was Charlie, with Laban's help, who built the stone-boat, a sort of sledge to haul wood. The place needed plenty of work, and Evie could see that McCloud was worried about them.

Using the stone-boat and one of the horses, they could haul good-sized logs, although they had snaked a few down before this, using simply a clove hitch near one end of a log. Over the years a lot of trees had fallen and limbs had been blown down, and there had been few campers to use it.

The stage now stopped at its own station, several miles away, so that source of income was finished. Now it was only themselves they could depend on, and what they could obtain from the country around. Evie carefully hoarded the few dollars saved from feeding the passengers, holding the money against a trip to the Plaza and a chance to buy warm clothing.

As Evie went outside she saw that the snow was falling faster, and a cold wind was blowing. Ruthie was gathering chips around the log where Laban chopped wood, and Evie took up the shovel and went back to the work of banking the cabin.

She was piling dirt around the foundation to keep the wind out and to make the house warmer. This was something they had done each year when she lived in the East, though there it was her father who had done it.

When she straightened up to rest her back, she looked off across the grassland toward the south. The far hills were no longer visible . . . the falling snow was drawing a curtain around them.

She went back to the work. She rarely thought of Jacob now, her life was too filled with planning, and doing. Sometimes she talked with the children about him, but his image had grown faint with the passing of time. He had been a stiff, unbending man who had loved his children, but he had never known how to show it to them, and Evie doubted if he ever felt the need to show them that he cared.

Their small herd had grown by two. Her cow had calved, and they had acquired another, a stray that wandered up to the water hole one day for a drink, and had just stayed with them. It wore no brand.

Suddenly she heard a long *halloo* and the pistol-like crack of a whip, and then she saw the racing stage team and the stage. It came plunging around the bend and down the little slope. Ben Logan was driving to-day, and he shouted at her. Somebody riding beside him waved, too, and then the stage was gone, disappearing in the falling snow.

She went back inside for a moment to add to the fire, putting on a few heavy sticks to keep the room warm while they were outside.

Just when she was growing worried about Laban, she saw the horse coming through the snow, and then the stone-boat, piled high with fire wood, and Laban walking beside it. When he came up to the cabin he tied the horse and came right over to her.

"Ma, we better watch out," he said. "I heard something back there. It sounded like a lot of riders or a lot of cattle."

"Did they see you?"

"I don't think so. I was down behind a tree digging a chunk out of the snow and frozen dirt, and the outfit was a few yards back of me in a grove where there was shelter from the wind.

"I didn't see but one rider, and I couldn't tell whether he was an Indian or a white man, but it looked as if he was riding a saddle. I just saw him shadow-like through the snow, and it sounded as if there might be a lot of them . . . or maybe not so many riders, but a lot of cattle. So I came on home."

"I'm glad you did." She turned. "Ruthie? Come on in. After Laban puts the horse up we will have a story and some doughnuts."

Who could the riders have been? It was not like Indians to ride in cold weather unless they were driven to it. Wisely, they preferred their lodges.

Outlaws? It seemed probable, for the route they were taking led to nothing but wilderness. Unless . . .

Two months ago, before the first snow had fallen, she had ridden back into the mountains, making a kind of sweep in a half-circle back of their place to see what fuel lay on the ground.

Drawn on by the silence as well as by the beauty of the hills, she had ridden six or seven miles into the mountains and had come upon a small park in the hills. It was a deep, grassy basin with forest around the edges and a few trees scattered across it. There was a stream there, and she noticed a dugout cabin in the side of the hill across the park. No smoke came from the chimney, and she saw no signs of occupation.

She went no nearer, but she did make a sweep around the end of the park and came on a dim trail. There were no fresh tracks, but there were old droppings of horses as well as of cattle, and some old tracks.

Whoever was driving these cattle that Laban had heard might know of that place.

She sat with the children around the fire, eating doughnuts, and Evie told them a story about her girlhood in Ohio and western Pennsylvania. When she looked out again she could barely make out the corrals. All was white and still, and cold.

When the story was finished and the children were working at the lessons she had laid out for them, she sat by the fire trying to plan for the coming weeks. There must be a path kept open to the shed and the corrals, the fuel must be used sparingly, and above all there must be enough work and amusement to keep the children busy.

Both of them would help in clearing the snow from the path, and both would help in bringing in the fuel. Laban would feed the stock. The worst of it was they did not have sufficient hay for a long hard winter. Part of the winter the animals must graze outside, pawing their way through the snow. This the horses could do, but the calves must be fed.

For three days the snow continued to fall, steadily and without letup. Every morning Laban went out at daybreak and shoveled snow to keep a path open to the shed.

The stock was in good shape. The snow banked the flimsy building and covered the roof with snow, so that inside it was warm and snug. Evie milked and carried the milk to the house, while Laban cleaned out from under the animals and put hay in their mangers.

The snow was more than two feet deep on the level, and was piled high on both sides of the path. The skies were now gray and overcast. The temperature was ten above zero on the thermometer beside the door.

"Ma!" Ruthie at the door tugged at Evie's arm. "Look!"

It was a wolf, a large gray wolf, almost white, on the side of the hill behind the cabin, watching them. He was not over fifty yards away, and was seemingly unafraid. Evie shouted at him, but he did not move. She turned back into the cabin. When she came out with the rifle the wolf was gone.

She thought about the men driving the cattle that Laban had seen or heard back there when the snow had started. They could not be honest men, driving where there was no trail, and in a direction where there was no town or ranch. It worried her that they should be so near.

Far to the south, Conn Conagher's horse floundered and fell. Stiff as he was, Conagher kicked loose from the stirrups and landed on his feet, then fell to his knees. He got up slowly, in time to help the gelding to its feet. Holding the reins, Conagher brushed the snow from his clothing.

The wind was on his cheek. It had been blowing right out of the north into his face. He turned the reluctant horse to face it, and then, holding the reins, he led off, struggling against the wind and deepening snow.

He didn't need anyone to tell him he was in trouble. So far as he knew, there was nothing ahead of him until he reached the stage road, which would be invisible in all this snow. Beyond it there was nothing but plains, mountains, and wilderness.

There was a cabin, though . . . shelter if he could reach it. That woman . . . what was her name? She ran a stage station that should lie almost due north of him. But Conagher recalled that somebody had said the stage had moved their station further west; in that case the woman was probably gone and the buildings abandoned.

Still, it would be shelter of a kind. But how far had he to go? And how far *could* he go?

Going back was out of the question. His horse was already played out, the snow was getting deeper, and there was, in this bare plain, no place to stop. There was no shelter from the wind, and the snow was too dry to build up a bank or to dig into it.

To go on until he could go no farther was dangerous, for with his body's resources drained, he would have no strength to resist the cold. He knew that most of those who freeze to death do so because they struggle too long. He could stop, huddle in a bundle, and try to wait out the storm, but although he might and probably would survive it, his horse would not. Their only hope was to go on, to try to reach some shelter where a fire could be built, and they could have protection from the wind and cold.

He never remembered when the wind fell. He had been struggling on, breaking trail for his horse for what seemed an interminable period, and suddenly he realized the snow was no longer blowing so much, the wind was dying down. Before him lay miles of white, unbroken snow. The trail of the stolen cattle lay under it.

He plodded on, holding a hand over his nose, trying to keep his scarf across his face. Once again the horse fell, slipping on an icy rock beneath the snow, and again Conagher got it up. Now he could see the low black line of the hills, with a star hanging low in the sky.

A star? No, it was a light. It had to be a light, as low as that. He closed his eyes, took two steps forward and opened them. The light was still there. He was not dreaming.

Evie was serving hot soup to the children when something fell against the door. Putting the soup down hastily, she went to the door, hesitated a moment, then opened it.

A snow-blurred, half-frozen man toppled into the room, fell to his knees, then struggled up.

"My horse," he mumbled, "my horse is out there."

"I'll get him," Laban said, and went for his coat and mittens. "I'll put him up."

"You'd better have some soup," Evie said practically, and guided him to a place on a bench, not bothering to remove his outer clothing. Let him get warm first. Her floor had been wet from melting snow before this, and on a dirt floor it would be a trouble only briefly.

She put soup into a bowl and spooned some of it into his mouth. After about the third spoonful, he stopped her and struggled to get off his gloves and his fur cap.

"Why, you're Mr. Conagher!" she exclaimed.

"I reckon so, ma'am. . . . That soup surely tastes

good." He started to rise. "Got to take care of my horse."

"Let Laban do it. He's very good with animals, and he'll like doing it."

After a while Conagher stood up and removed his sheepskin coat, and then sat down again to finish the soup.

"Two days," he said. "It's the first I've eaten in two days. My grub played out, but I had coffee until this morning. Tried to make some, but the wind blew out my fire, blew my coffee into the snow."

"Where did you come from?"

"Ranch south of here. Away down yonder."

Laban came in while Conagher was on his second bowl of soup. "I rubbed your horse down, sir. I am sorry we have no grain."

Conagher looked up and grinned. "You feed that mustang grain and he'd reckon you was tryin' to poison him. Thank you, son. That horse has come a far piece."

"It is bad weather to ride in."

"I was followin' some rustled cattle. Lost the trail in the snow."

Evie looked at Laban, and Conagher caught her glance. "You seen any cows?" he asked.

"Yes, sir, I saw some. I think they're being held in a corral over back of us, back in the mountains a few miles."

"How many men?"

"I don't know, sir. Maybe only a couple, but there might have been more."

"We could send word by the next stage," Evie suggested, "and the sheriff could ride over from the Plaza."

"Ma'am, those cattle would be clean gone out of the country by that time. No, ma'am, I figure the sheriff has a-plenty to do without me causing him trouble. I'll just mosey up there and start those cattle back home."

She was silent for a few minutes and then she said, "If you could wait we might get some help for you. It would only—"

"Mrs. Teale, a man who has to ask for help better not start out in the first place."

The heat was beginning to drive the cold from his flesh, slowly sinking deeper into his body, and as it did so he felt a vast comfort and a sense of ease and well-being come over him.

Even as he began to grow sleepy he became aware of the neatness of the cabin, the good manners of the children, and the quiet sense of security.

Evie Teale brought him a plate of beef and beans, and some baking-powder biscuits, and he ate, almost falling asleep in the process. When he had finished eating, Evie suggested that he unroll his blankets on the floor and sleep.

She stepped around him as she worked. He was a lean, powerful man, taller but not much heavier than Jacob. How black his stubble of beard showed against his face!

This was the man who had given Kiowa Staples that awful beating, but he did not look like a brutal man.

In the last hours of the night, she awoke suddenly and for an instant she lay quiet, wondering what had wakened her. She thought she had felt a cold draft . . . she sat up and looked toward where Conagher's bed had been.

It was gone, and Conagher was gone.

She lay down again, feeling a strange sense of loss, of loneliness . . . but that was foolish. He was nothing to her—just a strange, lonely, violent man, and she would not be likely to see him again.

12

Conn Conagher rode out in the morning, still tired though he had slept the night through on the dirt floor in the pleasantly warm cabin. But it had been almost too comfortable for him. When a man gets used to sleeping wherever he can spread himself, he soon gets to like it. When he left in the early hours before daylight he rode out because he simply felt more comfortable in a saddle than in a house.

It was cold. The gelding had humped its back against the saddle, liking the shelter of the shed, flimsy as it was, but Conagher knew what he had to do. Before he got up into the saddle he took out his pistol and gave the cylinder a spin or two and tried the action. Sometimes the oil will stiffen up when a gun has been out in the cold.

He tied his scarf around his face, tucked his ears under the earlaps, and rode into the trees. There was deep snow except where the wind had swept the hillside clear, and he was not expecting an easy time of it. But nobody likes to roll out at daybreak on a cold morning, and outlaws were even less likely to do it than working cowhands.

It took him two hours to struggle through the heavy snow to where he could look into the basin. He saw a hollow where the wide-spreading branches of a couple of big twin pines had kept the snow away and formed a sort of shelter. He swung down and left the horse there while he went out on a point and bellied down among the rocks.

With his field glass he studied the cabin below.

The cattle were there. At that distance he couldn't make out the brands, but a cowman soon learns to recognize individual cattle, just as a politician will recognize certain people in a crowd. These were Seaborn Tay's cattle.

Conagher studied the ground. As near as he could make out, there had been little movement around the dugout. A thin column of smoke came from the stovepipe that did for a chimney.

It seemed to be growing colder. Then Conagher realized that the wind was rising, coming right out of the north again. Well, that was good. This outfit wasn't likely to go anywhere with those cattle in this snow with a north wind rising.

He looked at the cabin again. He had no sympathy for those men down there. They were men not very unlike himself, but they had chosen to steal rather than to work, and Conagher was a worker who believed in an honest day for an honest dollar. He was going to take those cattle back to the ranch, and that was all there was to it.

He got up and went back to his horse. He considered a minute and then said aloud, "The hell with it," and swung into the leather.

He turned the gelding on an angle down the slope, keeping on the blind side of the dugout. He hoped there were no cracks in the walls, but it was likely that they had all been stopped up to keep out the cold.

He was feeling tough and mean with the cold weather and the hard travel. He wasn't hunting trouble, but he just didn't give a damn. Bringing a few branches from a cedar, he rode up to the cabin close to the chimney, which stuck out the side. When he came alongside the dugout he spoke softly to his horse and stood up on the saddle.

The gelding was well trained, and could be climbed on or over. Standing on the saddle, Conagher stuffed greenery into the stovepipe, then filled any spaces with some extra tufts of the cedar.

He dropped down to the saddle, moved to the corner of the dugout, and waited.

Suddenly there was an explosion of swearing and the door burst open, letting out a man in undershirt and pants with one boot on, the other in his hand. The other men piled out after him, coughing and swearing, driven from their warm beds by the smoke, all of them angry, none of them armed. Only one man had boots on.

"All right!" Conagher called. He put a bullet into the ground at their feet and charged his horse between them and the door of the cabin. One man, struck by the shoulder of the horse, went sprawling into the snow.

"Back up!" Conagher ordered. He held the rifle in one hand and with the gelding herded them back. One man made a dart to get around him, and Conn struck him a back-hand blow with the rifle barrel that stretched him out in the snow. "Get out there and take down the bars!" he said.

"I'll be damned if I will!" one man answered.

"You'll be damned if you don't!" Conagher cocked the Winchester. "You call it. I've had a damn long, cold ride, and I'd just as soon leave the three of you here for the wolves. Get on with it!"

One of the men started to move slowly, after a quick glance at the others, and the rest spread back, away from him.

Conagher turned his horse and rode at the gate, just

in time to see a man throw up a Winchester to take aim. He had been sleeping in the lean-to.

Conagher, holding low, let go with his rifle. His first shot burned the man and turned him, and Conagher fired again. He saw the rifle drop and, wheeling, he shot again, this time using both hands, and the man went plunging into the cabin door. He fell across the threshold, slowly drawing up one leg, and then he lay still.

Quietly Conagher said, "You boys better take down the bars."

And they did.

With his rifle he indicated one of the men. "You haze them out, then stand back."

When the cattle were outside, he told the men to line up, facing the pole corral, and had them put their hands against the top rail. He swung down then and went up to the wounded man in the corral and collected his guns.

A bullet had glanced off the lean-to doorpost and gone through the man's forearm, going in above the wrist and emerging near the elbow. His right hand was out of action, and was bleeding badly.

"Get out!" Conagher booted him in the rear and sent him out with the others. He thrust the man's six-shooter into his own waistband and put his Winchester into his saddle scabbard.

"You goin' to let me bleed to death?" the man pleaded. "For God's sake, man!"

"You fool around with the band wagon, son," Conagher told him, "and you're liable to get hit with the horn. You get up against the fence and be glad I don't gut-shoot you."

He backed off, and with a side swing knocked in the glass in the window of the shack. Most of the smoke from the fire was out by now, but he looked around, saw there was nobody inside, and collected the guns.

He threw their boots out into the snow. "Get 'em on," he said. To one of the men he said, "You help the man with the bloody arm. Better fix that arm up for him, too. A man bleeding like that's liable to freeze to death."

"What you doing to us?"

"Don't hurry me. I might decide just to shoot you instead of hangin' you, and I might turn you loose. I ain't made up my mind."

He glanced at the man who lay sprawled in the doorway. He had never seen him before. He had never seen any of these men, but three of them rode Ladder Five horses.

After making sure there were no more weapons, he threw their coats to them. Then he gave a look around the cabin, keeping the men in his line of fire.

There was a sack of canned goods, several slabs of bacon, and a sack of flour. He gathered them up and carried them outside away from the door; then he went inside and kicked the coals from the fire out into the room, and quickly stepped out. In a moment the cabin had caught fire.

"What in hell you tryin' to do?" The one who yelled at Conagher was a black-jawed man with a deep scar over one eye.

"This here place has been a hide-out for thieves long enough. I'm burnin' it out."

"What about our outfits?"

"The hell with you! You were free enough to steal ST cows. Get your outfits where you got your orders."

"Smoke will kill you for this," the black-jawed man said, "if I don't do it first."

"You open your mouth again until I tell you to," Conagher said mildly, "and you'll have a scar over the other eye."

He pointed to another of the men. "You saddle up for all of you, and be fast about it."

When the horses were saddled he told them to get on their horses and ride out. "The sheriff in the Plaza is just a-waitin' for you," he lied, "so your best bet is east."

"East? There ain't a town or place for fifty miles!"

"Tough, ain't it? Well, that's the life of an outlaw. You never know what's goin' to happen next. As a matter of fact, there's a couple of stage stations, but I'd fight shy of them, if I were you. All of them know that brand you ride for."

He gathered up their guns as they rode out and put them in a sack, then he put the supplies into another sack and loaded them on the dead man's horse.

Then he rode out, starting south, driving the cattle.

When the small herd came down the slope back of the Teale cabin, Evie, followed by Ruthie and Laban, came out to watch. The cattle gathered at the water hole and at the trough, and he rode up to the cabin. He swung down and took the bag of supplies from the back of the horse.

"Here's a couple of slabs of bacon, Mrs. Teale, and you can split the canned goods with me, and the coffee. You divide it up. I'll take one third to get me into the Plaza."

"This is very nice of you, Mr. Conagher, but I am afraid we can't pay—"

"Didn't ask you to. These here supplies were the wages of sin, ma'am, an' the woebegone sinners who pursued the path of Satan have seen the error of their ways. You take that grub and be glad."

He drew a six-shooter from the sack. "You keep this, too, you might have use for it."

"What happened, Mr. Conagher?"

"Nothing to speak of. Those sinners came upon evil

times, but if they're wise they are headed east now, and makin' good time."

He looked at her. "You got any of that soup left, Mrs. Teale? I'm a right hungry man."

After he had eaten, watching the road through the windows, just in case, he looked at Laban. "Boy, how'd you like to make a couple of dollars and a free ride on the stage?"

Laban glanced at Evie. "Well, sir, I'd like it. But what would I have to do?"

"Help me drive this herd to the Plaza. I'll pay you two or three dollars and your fare back on the stage."

"Is it all right, ma? Can I go?"

"Yes. Yes, you can. You'll take good care of him, Mr. Conagher?"

"Likely he'll take care of me. That's a fine, strong boy, Mrs. Teale, and he'll make a good hand."

When they reached the Plaza they bunched the cattle at the stockyards and put them in a pen.

At the livery stable the hostler looked sharply at the Ladder Five brand on the horse that Laban rode. "Now, see here—" he began.

"You see here," Conagher said. "I'm leavin' that horse for any Ladder Five rustler to pick up. And you can tell them that was the way I put it. The rider ain't likely to show up to claim it, and if he does you can go down to the saloon and tell those loafers you've seen a real honest-to-Abe-Lincoln ghost."

"You penned some cattle."

"Those are ST cows and I'm an ST rider, and in a few minutes I'm going to sell those cattle, give the buyer a bill of sale, and take a receipt. I'll be damned if I'll drive them all the way back to the ranch in this weather. Money is a whole lot easier to carry."

Conagher and Laban went across to the saloon,

which like all such saloons was a club house, an exchange for trail information, an auction or sales room, or whatever. At the door Conagher paused, glanced around, and saw Mahler sitting across the room. He walked in, and said to Laban, "You keep shy of me until we leave. A saloon is no place for a boy, but we've got business to do."

At the bar a squarely built man in a leather coat was watching them. Mahler looked up, his face stiffening into hard lines as he recognized Conagher.

Conagher approached the man at the bar. "Are you Tom Webb?"

"I am."

"I ride for the ST. I've got twenty-seven head of good stock down at the pens I'd like to sell. I'll give you a bill of sale and I'll want a receipt."

Webb hesitated. "I can use the cattle. But isn't this an odd time to sell?"

"This here," Conagher spoke roughly, and not quietly, "is recovered stolen stock. It's too far a piece to drive it back to the outfit."

Kris Mahler sat very still, staring into his beer glass. His face was drawn and cold. Conagher pointedly ignored him.

"What happened?" somebody asked.

Conagher shrugged. His sheepskin coat was unbuttoned and his gun hand was warm enough, warm as it would ever be. He did not want a shooting, but he just didn't care. He had ridden too far in the cold, he had been caused some rough work, and weariness had eaten into every bone and sinew.

"Trailed the cattle to a shack north of Mrs. Teale's place. I recovered the cattle, burned the shack, and drove the stock here."

"You *trailed* them? In this snow?"

Conagher looked at the speaker and said quietly, "I trailed 'em. Happens I knew about that shack, so when I lost the trail I knew they'd probably have to hole up there."

Nobody spoke for a few minutes, and then Webb said, "I'll walk over and look at the cattle."

"Any idea who the men were?" one man asked.

"Well, they were ridin' Ladder Five horses," Conagher said.

Kris Mahler shoved back his chair and got up. For a moment he stood, hands resting on the table, staring down. Then he turned abruptly and strode from the room.

13

With the coming of spring the wind blew cold and raw across the brown plains. Evie looked at the stock with fear in her eyes, for both horses and cattle were painfully thin. The past months had been hard. Bitter cold and frozen snow kept even the horses from finding grass beneath the snow's surface. Unless there was grass soon she would lose the few calves she had.

But there was no sign of green. It was the time when the sun should be warming the soil, it was the time for rains, but there was neither sun nor rain.

The food that had been left her by Conagher more than two months ago was gone. The stage had stopped once, with a broken wheel to be mended, and fortunately there had been enough food then to feed the passengers. She had a little money from that, but she hesitated to try the long trip to the Plaza with the horses in their present condition.

And both of the children were thin. Laban had shot a couple of squirrels, but there was scarcely a bit of meat on either, and now they were in serious trouble. The flour was gone, the sugar was gone. With the last of the bacon grease she had fried slices of bread for the children.

She knew she should kill one of the calves, but she had never butchered an animal and had not the slightest idea of how to go about it. Moreover, she hated to lose even one of her small herd. But it had come to that.

Twice she had planned to flag down the stage and get McCloud or Logan to bring her something from town, but each time she had missed the stage. This morning she was going out early, to be waiting beside the road when it came.

Much of the carefully hoarded money from feeding the stage passengers was already spent. She had needed a coat for Laban and mittens for all of them.

Far to the south Conagher saddled up and rode out. He had seen nothing of Parnell, and believed the lot of them had, for the time at least, left the country. There had been stage holdups on the road into Tucson, there had been others on the Black Canyon trail between Phoenix and Prescott. There had been a bloody attempt on the stage in the mountains near the Colorado, on the road to Hardyville.

Conagher swung wide now, checking for grass. There was none. Melting snow had frozen, and the stock could not break through. He opened up several water holes, found in a sheltered canyon some stock that was doing well, and then saw a patch of green up a canyon he had never entered.

He turned and started up the canyon, hoping to find grass. He had gone no more than half a mile when suddenly he saw, off to one side, dirt churned by the hoofs of shod horses. It was fresh . . . it had probably happened that morning. He swung his horse just an instant before the bullet struck.

He felt the slam of a bullet into his back and heard the report of the rifle as he toppled from the saddle. He fell, struck the ground on his shoulder, and rolled over. His horse went dashing on, and he knew instantly that they would be down here after him.

Fortunately he had carried his rifle in his right hand, hoping for a shot at a deer or antelope.

He caught the rifle up from the ground, and even as he heard a thundering of hoofs, he rolled over a slab of rock and slid a dozen feet to the bottom, where he crawled into a hole made by one rock toppled against another.

He scrambled through here quickly and down a steep dry watercourse, where he saw an opening and ducked into it. It was only a small space between rocks.

Behind him he heard a shout. "He's wounded, Smoke! We got him!"

For the first time he remembered that he had been knocked from the saddle by a shot. He was wounded then, and there must have been some blood. No doubt he was numbed from the shock, which meant that it would not be long before he would feel the pain, and perhaps would not be able to go any farther.

Before him was a tilted slab of rock shaped like a rooster's comb. He would be exposed on the face of it, but they were still out of sight around the corner, and there was a way a man might go where the face of the rock met the talus slope that fell away for several hundred feet. Gripping his rifle, he started to run. In an instant his brief respite was gone and the wound was throbbing with pain.

But he made it halfway along, and suddenly saw a place where two slabs of rock overlapped. The opening, which was V-shaped, was filled with stiff, wiry brush covered with thorns.

He had no choice. He could hear them coming, and once they rounded the rock back there he would be a clear target, caught against the face of the rock, a target that could scarcely be missed, in a place where there was no shelter. He dived at the stiff brush, fighting frantically to get past it.

Luckily, he had thrown himself on top of the brush, so he was squirming over it rather than trying to get through, which would have been almost impossible. He squirmed and scrambled, his breath coming in hoarse gasps of mingled pain and fear. Then he got hold of a large branch, and swung himself over into the space beyond, where he fell panting to the ground.

He lay there, stunned, his breath still coming raggedly, and for several minutes he could scarcely think.

When he looked around, he found himself in a sort of natural cup within a cluster of ragged peaks. It looked almost like a volcanic crater, though it was not.

There was not more than an acre of ground in the bottom of the hollow, with a thick covering of green grass. Against one wall there were some trees, and he could hear water rippling.

Painfully, he crawled across the little basin to the stream. The water was clear and cold.

He drank, and then lay on the ground beside the stream, where he must have passed out. When he awoke he was very cold, the sun had gone, and it was almost dark.

Despite the cold, he lay there trying to quiet the chattering of his teeth. He listened but he heard nothing.

Using the rifle as a crutch, he pushed himself up and half staggered, half fell into the edge of the trees.

After a few moments he began to gather some sticks together. Did he dare build a fire? There seemed little likelihood that the flames could be seen, and as for smoke, it was already night, and the chances were small.

With trembling fingers he shredded bark, added twigs, and lit a small fire, to which he then added some larger twigs. The light cheered him, and the warmth felt good.

Carefully, he looked all around him. The rock wall of one of the pinnacles was at his back, trees and brush were around him, and the basin, so far as he could see, was empty.

Thinking back, he recalled the twisted way he had come, and how he had emerged along the face of the jagged rock. No rider could have reached that place, and, looking up from below, they could not have seen the break between the overlapping rocks.

So he had vanished.

Would they come back in the morning to look? It was possible, even likely. But from here he could control the opening, and nobody was going to get in as long as ammunition and strength held out.

With careful fingers he felt of his back and found a deep gouge where a bullet, or a fragment of one, had entered the flesh slightly above his hipbone and had cut through the flesh along his ribs, just nicking the thick muscle before going off.

It was a painful wound, but not a serious one. He had lost blood, and it was going to hurt when he moved, for his side was badly bruised, and possibly some ribs were broken, though they did not feel like it.

The bullet must have glanced up from the cantle of his saddle. The cold and perhaps the thickness of his woolen underwear and shirt had stopped the bleeding for the time being.

He had no coffee, nothing. He drank a little water heated in a dish he made from bark, an old trick he had often used. The flames heated the water but did not burn the bark as long as they only touched it below the water level. The water inside absorbed the heat.

The hot water helped to warm him, and then he dug out a place among the leaves and pine needles, cowered deep within his sheepskin coat, and went to sleep.

He awoke shivering in the cold morning, with the last stars solitary in the vast darkness. He started to sit up, felt a twinge of pain, and lay still again. He was going to have the devil's own time of it, he could see that. He was miles from the ST headquarters, without a horse, without food, and wounded. Although the calendar said this was a month of spring, the weather gave no indication of it, and even a tenderfoot would have known he was in serious trouble.

After some struggle he got his fire going again. Fortunately there were a good many dry branches lying around, and there were the remains of a fallen tree and some pine cones. He could reach enough fuel to keep his fire going for some time without moving around too much. Once the flames leaped up, he eased himself into a sitting position, favoring his wounded side.

The effort left him gasping, and he sat still, letting the fire warm him, and reaching for an occasional stick.

If they came back they might find him, but they might not. The snow was gone from the top of the talus slope along which he had come, and the ground was frozen. He might have left no tracks on that frozen ground.

They might find some broken twigs where he had forced a way over the brush, but even that was a question. But did they need to find him at all? They knew he was wounded, they knew the cold was not over, and they knew how small is the chance of a wounded man, who has lost blood, in fighting off the cold.

They only needed to keep him bottled up here. They did not need to find him, and to run the risk of coming in after him, which would be like going into a den after a bear. They could just ride a patrol around the area and be sure he did not leave it.

Smoke Parnell had been out there. And the voice he had heard had sounded like that of Tile Coker . . . both tough men.

When he was warm enough to take an interest in his hideout, he looked around and assayed his situation. So far as he could see, there was only one opening, the one through which he had gained access. Because of the sheltered position, the grass had already begun to turn green, and there were leaf buds on the cottonwoods. On the far side of the hollow, where the sun reached only briefly, the snow had frozen into a bank of ice.

There was fuel enough at hand for some time, there was shelter in some of the rocky overhangs and there might be herbs with which he could treat his wounds. Using his left hand, he caught hold of a branch and pulled himself erect. Prowling along the slope, he found some cliff rose, a resinous, strong-smelling plant, sometimes called quinine bush. It was a plant important as winter browse for deer, cattle, and sheep; and judging by remnants he had found in caves, Conagher knew that the primitive pre-Indian peoples had used to braid the bark into sandals, rope, and mats. The Hopis used the wood for making arrows, but what was important for Conagher at the moment was that they used the plant to make a wash for wounds.

He gathered some of the bark, leaves, and smaller twigs and began to heat the lot in his improvised bark dish. When it had boiled, he stripped and, using his bandana and taking his time, bathed his wound with the decoction, his sheepskin over his shoulders to keep him from getting too chilled.

Whether it did any good he was not sure, although he knew that the Hopis swore by it. After that he wandered about, found some dry spectacle pod, crushed it to powder, and put it on the wound, another remedy used by both the Hopi and Tewa Indians.

After an hour or so of lying beside the fire, he began to think more about food. Conagher was a man who had often missed meals. Going hungry was not a new experience, though not a pleasant one, but food was a necessity now if he was to recover and regain the strength it would take to get him out of this situation.

Animals and birds must know of this place, he thought. Men, if they had ever discovered it, had left no signs here. But if animals came here, he should be able to trap or kill one for food.

After a time he got up and moved his camp to the overhang. This had the advantage of bringing him within range of a new supply of fuel. Sitting by the fire, he carefully studied the plants within range of his eyes. Meanwhile he chewed on a couple of leaves from the salt bush. How much food value they possessed he had no idea, but they gave him the satisfaction of chewing and the taste was pleasant.

He was very thirsty and went often to the stream to drink. He saw rabbit droppings near the water and the tracks of several small animals in the sand near the stream.

After a while he lay down again, feeling very tired. It was only with an effort that he could replenish his fire, but he kept it alive. The wood was dry and gave off almost no smoke.

He slept, but awoke suddenly, feeling the chill of

night. Evening had come and his fire had burned itself down to gray ash. Only one small branch still glowed. He fed it gingerly with tiny bits of shredded bark, then with twigs.

Conagher stripped off his shirt and, hanging the coat over his shoulders for warmth, bathed his wound again with hot water and cliff rose, then powdered it with the crushed spectacle pod.

After he put on his clothes he walked with great care down to the bank of the stream. In the brush close by he rigged a couple of snares, and then went over to the notch through which he had crawled.

Peering out, he could see only a patch of sky, and below it the darkness where the earth lay, the valley below the rim where he had taken refuge.

Kneeling down, he began with his bowie knife to cut the brush away so that he could tunnel through to the other side. He would work a few minutes, then stop to rest and to listen. Once he believed he heard movement, but when he continued to listen for a long time there was no further sound. After a while, having scarcely made a dent in the clump of brush, he went back to his camp, added fuel to the fire, and lay down, huddling as much of him as possible under the sheepskin coat.

He slept, dreaming wild dreams, and he awoke in a cold sweat. His side hurt him and he wanted to change his sleeping position, but every movement hurt, so he lay quiet listening to the leaves whispering and the subtle movements of small creatures. When morning came his snares were empty.

On this day he chewed some of the leaves from the salt bush, drank water from the stream, slept, and woke again. He found and ate some juniper berries, and rigged another snare.

In the night he awoke, built up the fire, and huddled

near it with the back wall of the overhang as a reflector that threw the heat back toward him. His head ached and he was very tired, but he did not feel like sleeping. He heated water, crushed some of the juniper berries into it, and drank the liquid. He had heard that the Hopis sometimes made a tea from juniper berries. After a while he slept again, and when he awoke it was raining.

For a time he huddled over his fire, his feeling of irritation growing. Finally he lurched to his feet, moved everything inflammable away from the fire, and taking his rifle, went back to the opening.

Listening, he heard nothing. Then he hacked at the wall of thorny brush until a partial opening was made. He had started to go through, then stopped, went back and tore down his empty snares. He wanted nothing to be trapped there to die uselessly.

He forced his way through the brush, paused, and listened, but he heard nothing except the soft fall of rain.

Weak though he was, he had decided that to stay here longer would only mean that he would grow weaker. He worked his way along the comb-like ridge, and found a place where he could climb down slowly and painfully.

Off to the right he saw what seemed to be the glow of a fire, and he started toward it. He needed food and he needed a horse, and he would be damned if he was going to go without them when his enemies—if that was who they were—had both.

Judging by the stars, it was past midnight when he came close to the fire. It was burning brightly under a crudely made shelter.

First he noted where the horses were tied, and then he saw his own horse there among them. Evidently they had found the horse running loose on the prairie, and had roped and kept it.

He looked around the camp. There were three men there, two of them in their beds, sleeping; the other was dozing beside the fire.

Conn Conagher was weak as a cat, but he was mad clear through. He had a bitter anger that drove him recklessly, and he did not hesitate. He walked right into the camp, kicked the rifle away from the hands of the man who dozed, and put a bullet into the ground between the two sleeping men.

One of them was young Curly Scott, the other was Smoke Parnell himself. The man by the fire was Pete Casuse.

The two sleeping men jerked erect and Conagher held the gun on them. "Damn you, Smoke," he said, "if I wasn't weak as a cat I'd beat you within an inch of your life. Now you lay right there, and you make a move, even to scratch, and so help me, I'll put a bullet in your belly.

"You," he said to Casuse, "dish up a plate of that grub, and hurry."

"Si." Casuse started to rise.

"Stay where you are. Just reach over and ladle it up, and use your right hand. I never shot a man who wasn't holding iron, but right now I just don't give a damn."

He lowered his rifle, slid his six-gun into his hand, and proceeded to feed himself with his left hand.

"I hope you try something," he said grimly. "I just hope you do. I'd like to bury the three of you right on this spot.

"Now, Smoke," he said, "I'm going to ride out of here. You boys are then going to get up and leave the country, and if you stop this side of Tascosa or Trinidad, you're crazier than I think you are. You've had your try at me and you failed, but as of noon tomorrow I'm hunting you, and I'm going to shoot on sight, without any warning whatsoever. I am going to ride your sign until you've killed me or I've put lead in all of you."

Parnell stared at him. "You're loco! You're plumb, completely loco!"

"Maybe . . . but you've given me grief, and I'll take no more from any man. All I'm going to give you is a running start."

He finished the plate of food and threw down the plate, then he drank three cups of coffee. Parnell made a slight move, and a bullet burned his shoulder.

Conagher swore. He had meant to hit him, but it was evidence of his weakness that he had missed. "You," he said to Casuse, "you get my horse and saddle up, and don't try anything foolish."

Moving slightly to keep the Mexican under his eyes, he watched him saddle up and carefully tighten the girth.

Conagher then moved around to pick up the reins with his left hand. His grip on the gun was very weak. Parnell was watching him.

"Hell," the outlaw said, "you're so weak you can scarcely stand."

"You want to see how weak? Reach for your gun."

"No," Parnell said practically, "because you've got just sand enough left in you to kill me."

Conagher turned, reached for the pommel, but never made it. He felt his knees giving way under him, grabbed at a stirrup, and it slipped through his fingers. He hit the ground on his face and lay still.

For a long moment nobody moved. Pete Casuse stared at Conagher, then looked at Smoke briefly. "There lies a man," he said, and then he glanced again at Parnell. "What was that town you were tellin' me about? Was it Milestown?"

"Up Montana way," Parnell said, "and I think that's a good idea."

He hesitated a moment, then threw back the blankets, sitting still until he was sure Conagher was not going to move.

Fascinated but frightened, Curly Scott was staring at the fallen man, and then he looked at Smoke. "Are you going to kill him?"

"Kill *him?*" Smoke Parnell turned around sharply. "Kid, you don't know what you're sayin'. I may be an outlaw, but I never yet murdered anybody in cold blood, least of all an hombre. And there, as my friend Casuse will agree, is an hombre that *is* an hombre."

"What are we going to do?"

"We—me an' Pete—we're ridin' back to the outfit and we're going to pick up Kris and Tile and we're heading for Montana. We're ridin' north with the spring."

"What about me?" Scott protested.

"You stay with him. When he's well enough to ride, take him back to Seaborn Tay. He's worth more to this country than that whole outfit. And while you're with him, kid, you watch him. If you ever get to be half the man he is, you come back and ride with me if you think you're still cut out for an outlaw."

When they were gone, Curly Scott stirred up the fire and started to drag the unconscious man closer. Then, worried at what he might do if he woke up, he just eased him onto a ground sheet, covered him over with blankets, and sat down to wait for daybreak.

Several times he turned to look at the sleeping man. He was dirty and unshaven, and his clothes were worn and bloody, but there was something about him, even in sleep, that spoke of what kind of a man he was.

Conagher stirred restlessly, muttering something about the wind in the grass.

"Tumbleweed . . ." he murmured, *"rolling like wheels . . . like wheels . . ."*

The words made no sense to Scott, but then, when did words spoken in delirium ever make sense?

14

Two weeks after his return to the ST, Conagher was riding again. He had wanted to go back to work after two days, but Tay would have none of it.

"You lay up for a while. Get some rest. Thing like that takes more out of a man than he knows."

Conagher mended a bridle, fixed the hinges on the corral gate, sank some post holes for a fence around the kitchen garden, and generally kept busy.

He had lost a lot of blood and he had missed some meals, but such things were all in the day's work. He had never had it easy, and did not expect to now. Johnny McGivern had stayed on, and they had hired Curly Scott, whose sister had gone on to California without ever seeing him.

March came to an end and April passed, and the grass was green from the spring rains, the prairies covered with wildflowers. The stock was fat and lazy, and Conagher rode wide, once even stopping by the Ladder Five, but the buildings were deserted and still, and tumbleweeds were piled against the corral after the spring winds.

Conagher swung the dun horse and walked him over to look at the tumbleweeds. Sure enough, there was something grayish-white on one of them near the bottom. Conagher pulled the tumbleweeds away until he could get at the note.

It was an old note, and must have been written late in the fall. It could scarcely be read, it was so faded.

> It is very cold, and I am often alone
> here. How I wish someone would come!

He read it and re-read it, then tucked it away, folded in a little bundle with the others. There was no accounting for what a lonely person would do; he knew that of his own experience. He was often alone, and like all men who rode alone he often talked to his horse. You got cabin fever after a while when you lived alone, and you just had to talk, and this was a lonely woman somewhere away off up north who needed to talk to somebody.

He prowled around the Ladder Five for a while. Nobody had been there for quite a while. In fact, they must have pulled out right after that time in the mountains. He had come out of it himself to find only young Scott with him, who had fixed him up some chow and they ate there together until they rode back to the ST.

As he rode away he turned in the saddle to look back. The Ladder Five was a good layout. Nobody owned it. Parnell and his outlaws had just squatted there, fixed things up enough to get along, and stayed on.

The ranch lay in a small cove in the rock wall of the mountain, with a few trees behind it and a clump off to one side that would break the wind. The house was solid and there was a good supply of water. The grass was green and the range lay out before it. Taken altogether, it was the sort of place where an honest man could do well by settling.

Several times during his ride back to the ST headquarters, Conn took out the notes and read them over. They didn't say much when you came right down to it, but they told of a lonely girl somewhere far off. Likely she didn't see many folks, stuck out on the plains.

Conagher rode up to the bunk house and got down and began throwing his duffel together.

Leggett came from the barn and watched him without comment for a few minutes, and then he said, "You lightin' a shuck?"

"Uh-huh."

"The Old Man will be some put out. He sets store by you."

"He's a good man."

"You better talk to him. He wants to make you foreman. He told me so, and it's right he should. You saved his outfit for him."

"I did my job."

"You done more. You done more than anybody could have expected."

Conagher straightened up. "Mister, when I hire on for a man, I ride for him. I ride for his outfit. If I don't like things I quit. I've got me a horse and a saddle and there's a lot of country I ain't seen, but when a man hires me I figure he hires my savvy and what all I can do."

"You run those outlaws clean out of the country."

Conagher shook his head. "I'd not say that. I just worried them to where it wasn't what you'd call comfortable for them. Nobody likes to laze it around more than an outlaw, and you keep him stirred up and he'll usually move. Well, I sort of stirred them up."

When his blankets were rolled and his gear packed he went up to the house and asked the cook for coffee. Seaborn Tay came in and dropped into a chair. "How's the range look?"

"Good. There was a good fall of snow and most of it

sank right in. No runoff to speak of. I'd say you'd a mighty handsome year ahead." He sipped his coffee. "Mr. Tay, I want to draw my time."

"Now see here, Conagher. You can't just up and leave a man that way. I need you. I was figurin' on you for foreman. I'm not as spry as I should be, and like you maybe guessed, I've got a bad heart. I'll give you a hundred a month."

"Nope."

"Look, where are you going to find that much? You've been riskin' your neck for thirty a month and you deserve to get more. I'll tell you what I'll do. I'll give you a hundred a month and a ten per cent share."

"I want to ride north. I got business up there."

Tay argued quietly, but Conagher merely sipped his coffee. The cook put a piece of pie before him, and he ate it.

"Things work out, I may be back. But I'll be back to lay claim to the Ladder Five. I won't be workin' for you, but I'll be your neighbor."

"You got a girl somewhere? You gettin' married?"

"I can't say. I've never been married, and don't figure I'm the sort to stand hitched."

Well, when it came to that, he didn't know. Somehow, when girling time came around he was always too backward, or else he was off riding the range where you couldn't find a girl. Other men no better off than he was had found some pretty fine women, here and yonder . . . and some miserable ones, too. It kind of scared a man.

He was no youngster any more, and it was no time to start building fancies, yet when it came to that, why not?

Anybody could dream, and it seemed to him that girl who'd been tying those notes to tumbleweeds had been doing a sight of dreaming. So he would just ride north, camp along the way, and kind of look the country over. When he came to a lonely cabin he'd find that girl, all right. He would know her anywhere.

It puzzled him how she lived, but he decided she was the daughter of some rancher, or maybe of a dirt farmer, or even, perish the thought, a sheepman's daughter.

He finished his coffee, pocketed the money Tay gave him without so much as counting it, and went outside. Tay followed him to the door.

"Damn it, man," he said, "why do you have to go tomcattin' off across the country? You could build yourself into a nice place here, and rightly a piece of it is yours."

"I'll be back some spring, follerin' the wild geese," Conagher said, and swung into the saddle. He lifted his hand to Leggett and McGivern, alone in the bunk house now that Euston was gone, and he rode away.

The grasslands looked greener in the distance than they did close up. He guessed it was always that way.

15

It was a fool thing he was starting out to do. He was going to try to find the girl who was writing those notes. It was foolish to try, because it was about as impossible a task as a man ever set for himself, but it was doubly foolish because what that girl was pining for was a young man, a man younger than Conn Conagher.

He looked at himself with no illusions. He was a hard-grained man, a man who had lived a hard life, and no great beauty to begin with. He carried scars, inside as well as out, and about all he had left was some years of hard work and a boy's dream of the girl he would find some day.

Oh, he had it, all right! Conagher considered himself with sour humor. He was a damn fool who should have outlived all that nonsense years ago. Maybe it was the fault of having read too much of Walter Scott while still not dry behind the ears.

So here he was, riding north across the plains looking for a will-o'-the-wisp. He checked out every piece of old tumbleweed he saw, but found no messages. He camped at night wherever he could find a good place.

When a week had gone by without finding a single message, he rode off the plains and headed toward the Plaza. There, in Callahan's, he met Charlie McCloud.

"I'll buy the drinks," McCloud offered.

"No, that's block and tackle whiskey. You take a drink, and then you walk a block and you'll tackle anything. I'm going to sit with you and have a beer."

"From what Smoke Parnell says, you don't need whiskey. You'll just tackle anything, any time."

"You've seen him?"

"I saw him when he was pullin' his freight for Montana. He said a decent outlaw couldn't make a livin' with you around."

"He's a tough man."

McCloud glanced at him. "Didn't I see you with a blanket roll behind your saddle? Are you drifting again?"

"I've got tumbleweed fever."

"You too?"

"What d' you mean—me too?"

"Seems to me half the cowhands in the country are hunting tumbleweeds these days. Somebody found a note tied to one, and that started it."

Conagher felt a swell of irritation within him. "Note? What kind of a note?"

"From some girl up north—at least, she's probably up north. She's been writing little notes or poetry or something and tying them to tumbleweeds. Just goes to show what happens when you're too long alone."

"How do you know she's alone?"

"The notes sound like it. The cowhands over east of here are makin' bets on whether she's short and fat, tall and skinny, a blonde or a brunette."

"She's probably got a husband who's broader across the shoulders than he is between the eyes," Conagher said dryly. "They better leave it lay."

"I don't know. Anyway, it's got them all stirred up. If she keeps it up, all the cow outfits in the country will be shorthanded."

Conagher traced circles on the table top with his beer glass. He was annoyed. Couldn't a man even have a dream by himself? But he should have guessed there would be others who found those notes.

"How far north have they found them?" he asked.

"I don't know. All across the country, I guess. I've only talked to them along the stage lines."

"A tumbleweed can roll a mighty long way. Hell, that woman may be married and have two kids since she wrote those notes. How you going to tell how old the notes are?"

Conagher signaled for a refill. "Speakin' of a woman with two kids," he said, "how's that Mrs. Teale gettin' along?"

"Had a hard winter, I guess. I haven't seen or talked to her in three, four weeks. I've seen them around when the stage rolls by . . . they always wave."

"Wonder what ever happened to her husband?"

McCloud shrugged. "He was carrying money. Four hundred in gold, she told me. Now, you know a man can't just carry money like that unless he's careful. But there's a lot could have happened. How many men have you known who rode off and just disappeared?

"A few years ago," he went on, "we found an empty stage out on the plains with nobody aboard, the horses feeding along the road, the driver and the two passengers gone. We never did figure out what happened. Maybe they all got out to look at something, or to walk up a steep grade, and something scared the team and they ran off . . . there's a lot could have happened. You know about how long a man can last in this country without a horse and without water."

In the morning Conagher rode east riding slow, checking the tumbleweeds as he went. They were old tumbleweeds, left over from the previous year, and on the one paper he found, the message had been erased by snow and rain.

After four days he saw to the north a thin column of smoke rising that he knew was on the Teale place, and he swung his horse and rode in that direction.

He had gone no more than fifty yards when he saw the trail of at least a dozen riders, going east. The grass was only now springing back into place; they must have gone by within the hour. Off the trail and keeping to low ground, as low as you could find in this almost flat plains country, he went on. Because of the grass, he could find no distinctive prints, but they seemed to be unshod horses.

"Well, boy," he said to the horse, "I reckon you better build a fire under your heels. We got some travelin' to do!"

He lifted the horse into a gallop, standing in the stirrups from time to time to get a better view of the country. He was close to the Teale place now, and all was quiet there. He could see the boy in the yard cutting wood; he could see him swing the axe, see it fall . . . and then an instant later he heard the sound.

He closed in at a hard gallop, swung into the yard and wheeled his horse. "Laban, where's your ma and sister?"

"Hi, Mr. Conagher! They went up the draw to pick greens. What's the matter?"

"Get in the cabin and stand by for a fight. There are Indians around. I'll get the womenfolks!"

He slicked his Winchester from the scabbard, saw the boy dart for the cabin, and then he went up the draw at a pounding run.

Evie and Ruthie were coming back, and he wheeled around. "Quick! Get a foot in a stirrup, one on each side! Hurry!"

"What's wrong?" Evie asked.

" 'Paches," he said shortly, and took them back down the draw and wheeled up to the cabin. "Get in, fast," he said.

He turned the horse and trotted it to the gate, then swung down, swung the gate open, and led the dun into the shed. He was hurrying toward the cabin when he heard the Indians coming. It was too late to make the cabin, though he saw two gun muzzles showing from loop holes, and knew the Apaches would see them, too.

They had swung around to the east and approached the cabin walking their horses. He counted eleven, all braves. He had stopped near the door, but out of line with the loop holes.

One of the warriors he knew by name, at least three of them by sight. Benactiny, often called Benito, was a great warrior, and a fighting man with more than usual wisdom.

"Hello, Benito," Conagher said casually. "You boys are pretty far north, aren't you?"

"These mountains"—Benactiny swept his hand toward the Mogollons—"were Apache medicine ground. This is our place."

"This is a time of change," Conagher said conversationally. "I heard you were livin' in the Sierra Madres, in Mexico."

"I live there," the Indian replied sullenly. "Too many white soldier come."

"Soldiers never worried Benito," Conagher said. "Nobody could drive Benactiny and his warriors. Benactiny went because he wished to go. He went to the lonely mountains where there was running water and many trees. He has been happy there."

Benactiny's expression did not change. He was a proud man, as Conagher knew. "You are right," the Apache said. "Nobody could drive Benactiny, but this is my land, too."

"Once it was your land," Conagher admitted, and then slyly, his expression innocent, he added, "Once it was Mimbres land."

"We took it from the Mimbres," Benactiny replied proudly.

"And then you went away and the white man has come. There are many white men, and they still come. They are as many as blades of grass upon the Plains of St. Augustine, and for everyone who dies, five will rise in his place.

"I hope not many die," Conagher added, "for I like the country as it is, with not too many people."

Benactiny changed the subject. "You are the man here? There was only a woman and two young ones."

"They are my friends. I watch over them. Their friends are my friends, their enemies are my enemies. It is good that you come in peace, for I would like to believe Benactiny is their friend as well as mine."

Benactiny studied him, the faintest shadow of a smile in his eyes, for before this the two men had barely spoken in passing, although each knew much about the other.

"I think you speak of peace," Benactiny said. "Is it that you are afraid?"

"You speak in jest." Conagher used the word he had heard an Army officer use to an Apache. "I have no need to fear. I have no enemies."

"No enemies?"

"I had enemies, but I have buried my enemies upon many hills. A man needs enemies to keep him wary and strong, but I would not have Benactiny for an enemy. I have spoken to all the white men of what a great warrior he is, but what a fine chieftain also. It is one thing to be fierce in battle, but it is important, also, to be wise in council."

Benactiny swung his pony. "We will ride on."

"Wait!" Conagher lifted a hand. "My friend Benactiny rides far. I would not have him ride without tobacco."

With his left hand Conagher delved into his saddlebag and came up with several sacks of Bull Durham. One he gave to Benactiny, and half a dozen others to the other warriors. "Divide them," he said, "and when you smoke, remember Conagher, your friend."

Deliberately then, he turned his back and stepped up to the door. It opened before him and he stepped in, reaching up with his left hand to take the saddlebags from his left shoulder. Then he went to a loop hole to peer out. The Apaches were riding away.

"They would have attacked us," Evie said.

"I think so."

"What did you say to them?"

He shrugged. "They're reasonable enough. I've fought Indians. I've fought the Sioux, the Cheyennes, the Apaches, the Comanches and the Kiowas, but I've shared meat with them, swapped horses with them, and found them reasonable men. They respect courage. You can't yield to an Indian. He will kill you out of contempt as much as for any other reason, but he respects courage, and he respects a good argument."

"He knew you."

"Let's say he recognized me. I ain't much, Mrs. Teale, but I'm too dumb to know when I'm whipped. He knew I'd fight just as I knew he would. We recognized that much in each other."

"Will you stay for supper? We were just gathering some greens."

"Well, I'll stay if you'll let me contribute. I've just come from the Plaza, a few days back, and I've got some bacon, a package of raisins, and a couple of pounds of prunes you might use. And I've got coffee."

"Thank you, Mr. Conagher. I will accept them. As a matter of fact, we are just out of coffee."

"Fry up some of that bacon," he suggested. "I'll go see to my horse."

She had said they were out of coffee, but Conagher had a hunch they were out of a lot of other things as well. All of them looked gaunt . . . they might not have missed meals, but the meals they'd had must have been pretty skimpy. How Evie Teale kept going without a man he could not guess.

He rubbed his horse down, forked some hay into the corner of the corral, then carried his saddle under the shed. He took his rifle, rope, and blanket roll to the cabin.

There was a lot of work around here that needed a man to do. The boy wasn't up to it yet. Conagher stopped up a leak in the water trough, and fixed a place on the roof where the wind had worried a corner loose, and when it was close to sundown he got his rifle.

"I'll be an hour," he said. "If I haven't got a deer

by then it'll be no use waiting longer. They've not been hunted, and they should be feeding down toward water about now."

He remembered the country from before. A western man habitually noted water holes and animal sign as he traveled through the country, and Conagher had crossed that ridge before. He got up on it, about thirty yards from the water hole with the wind in his face, and he lay down in the brush and waited.

Sure enough, scarcely half an hour had passed before he saw a deer, then two more. He chose a big buck, settled down with his aim on a neck shot. At that range he could not miss. He killed the buck, skinned it, and then loaded the meat in the hide and carried it back to the cabin.

He could smell the coffee, and the bacon was frying.

When he brought the meat into the cabin the first thing he noticed was Laban's slicked-down hair. Ruthie had tidied herself up, and so had Evie Teale. The table had a red and white checkered cloth on it, and it was all set and proper. Suddenly he was self-conscious.

He was unshaven for days, and he had been sleeping out wherever he could find a place. He had not paid much attention to anything more than combing his hair and washing up a mite.

"I'll wash up," he said. "Excuse me."

He stripped off his coat and shirt, rolled up his sleeves and washed, combed his hair by guess work in the piece of flawed mirror alongside the kitchen door, then shook out his shirt, put it on, and came back in.

"Sorry, ma'am," he said, "it's too dark to shave."

"That's quite all right, Mr. Conagher. Please sit down."

After his own cooking, any food tasted good, but this was excellent. There were two slices of bread on the table and he was eating the second before he suddenly realized there was none for anyone else. He ate the piece in silence, cursing himself for being a fool.

"You've got a nice place here," he commented. "I see you have some calves."

She explained about the cattle. "Better let me brand them for you, Mrs. Teale. There will be other herds coming through, and unbranded cattle surely have a way of coming up missing."

"I'd be pleased, Mr. Conagher."

When he got up to walk outside after supper, Evie glanced around at him. He was certainly a fine figure of a man when you really looked at him. He was tall, with wide shoulders, and he had an easy way of moving that was more like a woodsman than a rider. And he seemed sure of himself without in any way appearing bold.

There had always been the shadow of worry under Jacob's seeming assurance, and she was sure that Jacob, deep inside, had never really believed in himself. He was prepared for failure despite the fact that he was so stern, so hard-working, and so demanding of dignity.

She knew next to nothing about Conn Conagher, only that he was reported to be a top hand who asked no favors of anyone, a grim, hard man . . . a man to leave alone, as McCloud had said.

She knew he had ridden into the back country and brought back cattle that belonged to the ranch he worked for, cattle that he must have taken back from some pretty dangerous men. Yet he seemed strangely shy, and gentle. Though that had been true of several men she had met who were reputed to be dangerous.

She made her bed upstairs with the children, and Conagher slept on the floor.

When she awoke in the morning and saw that he was gone, she was suddenly frightened. It had been so reassuring to have him here, and she realized that for the first time in months she had slept soundly.

She was dressing when she heard the sound of a gun, and then another. She managed to get down the ladder and get water on for coffee before he came.

"Shot a couple of turkeys," he said. "They're in good shape."

All that day Conagher worked around the place, and he kept thinking of the girl who wrote the notes tied to the tumbleweeds. If he was going to find her he knew it was time he started on, but he stayed to brand the calves, he helped Laban with some heavy logs well back on the ridge, and he killed another deer.

"You can jerk the meat," he said, and showed her how to cut it into thin strips for drying.

Twice he rode out, studying the country around. Jacob Teale had picked a poor place to settle, and would have failed here as he had elsewhere. There wasn't enough grass in the nearby meadows to cut for hay, and the grazing was not as good as on the old Ladder Five range.

One evening Evie was coming in from milking and he was sitting on the stoop watching the sun set on the hills. "It is very beautiful, Mr. Conagher," she said. "I like to watch the wind on the grass."

He started to answer that, and then stopped. Kris Mahler was riding into the yard.

16

Mahler pulled up when he saw Conagher, and the expression on his face was not one of pleasure.

"I figured you'd pulled your freight," he said. "I heard you quit the Old Man." His horse side-stepped a little, and when he straightened him out again he went on, "A lot of good it did you, riskin' your neck for him. There's a couple of good men gone because of it."

"Not because of what I did," Conagher replied; "because of what they tried to do. As for what good it did me, I was just doing my job, the way I'll always do it."

"You think I didn't do mine?"

"You can answer that question best yourself. You ran out on the Old Man when he needed you. You joined up with his enemies."

"That's a damn lie!"

"There was a time when I'd have reached for a gun if a man said that to me," Conagher said, "but you know whether I'm lyin' or not, and I know it, so what you say doesn't make a bit of difference."

Mahler stared at him, his expression cold and mean. "I never liked you, Conagher," he said. "You're not my kind of man."

"I take that as a compliment."

Mahler turned his horse sharply and rode away. Conagher watched him go, then turned to Evie Teale. "I am sorry for that, Mrs. Teale. I believe he came to see you."

"It doesn't matter."

After a moment she said, "I was surprised, Mr. Conagher. They told me you were a quarrelsome man, yet you avoided trouble."

"I don't want to fight him. He's a top hand when he works, a good man who is on the verge of being something else. But you were present," he said. "I wouldn't want to fight with a lady present."

"Thank you."

They walked to the cabin together, and he held the door for her. After she went in he sat down on the stoop again.

The last of the sun was gone, and the first of the stars had come. The night wind was bending the grass, and his eyes studied the hills. There was something restful in this, sitting here in the evening, the day's work done, the sounds of supper being prepared inside, the low murmur of voices. It was something he'd missed . . . how long since he had lived in a house with a woman in it?

"Not since I left home," he said to himself, "not since I left my aunt and uncle when I was fourteen."

Grading camps, cow camps, mining camps . . . the women you found there weren't his kind. He was a lonely man who did not make up to people easily. It came hard. When he was with women he never thought of anything to say. It seemed as if all he knew was stock, range conditions, and the stories of some fights, and these didn't add much to his conversation.

He felt that he should be saddling up and riding on —it was no good staying here. Yet he did not move. He watched the stars come out, and thought of Mahler.

The man had a burr under his saddle about something. About a lot of things, maybe. Why hadn't he gone with Smoke? Why had he stayed behind?

An idea came to Conagher, but he shied away from it. Kris Mahler had nothing against him . . . or shouldn't have. Still, he was riding it rough tonight. Had he been trying to pick a fight? Or was he sore because he found Conagher here?

Was he sweet on Evie Teale? When you came right down to it, she was a fine-looking woman. A nice shape to her, and pretty, too.

Well, she *was* pretty. Maybe not to everybody's taste, but she was to his. She was a handsome woman, he thought. And it took sand to stay on a place like this with two kids, and no money coming in. It took real old-fashioned grit.

By rights he should saddle up in the morning and pull out. If he was ever going to track down the girl who wrote those notes he was going to have to do it before his money gave out, or before somebody else got there first.

He told himself he would get going in the morning, but he did not feel very positive about it.

The trouble was, he suddenly realized, that he was comfortable, and he could not remember how long ago it had been since he was comfortable.

The door opened suddenly. "Mr. Conagher, supper is ready," Evie said.

All through supper he sat there wanting to say something and he couldn't find the words. Finally he said, "I reckon I'd better drift. I can't sponge off you forever."

"You've helped," Laban said. "I can't shoot straight enough to kill much game. We never had turkey before."

"Sometimes you can kill them with a club. I've seen it done."

Evie Teale stared at him, but when he looked up she glanced away quickly, blushing for some reason he could

not imagine. "I know you must have much to do," she
said. "I . . . you have helped us."

She looked at him suddenly. "We were having a
bad time, you know."

He took out some money—not that he had so much
left after laying in the supplies he had bought. "Look,
I'll be coming back this way. Maybe you'd better take
this so you'll have something for me to eat when
I come back.

"I mean, I don't want to pay you, but I want to feel
free to come back."

"You don't have to leave money," Evie said. "You
can come any time. We hope you will." Then, not to
seem too forward, she added, "We don't have much
company now that the stages do not stop here. It is
very lonely."

"Yeah . . . sure, it must be."

He rode out in the morning. At the last he did not
want to go and he waited, wanting her to ask him to
stay, not knowing whether he dared say anything about
it to her. Why had he been such a damn fool as to say
he was leaving? He had no reason to leave, when it
came right down it to. He was just going hunting
tumbleweeds . . . what kind of a silly idea was that,
anyway?

Was he a kid to go dreaming about some fancy prin-
cess or something? Some beautiful girl who was held
prisoner somewhere? What was he thinking of?

All right, suppose those notes did say something to
him? That was no reason to be a fool. He wasn't a kid
any more.

If he had any brains he would turn right around and
go back, but he kept riding on. He was riding east, and
he wasn't even looking at the tumbleweeds. Twice he
passed places where they were piled along the brush-
lined road, but he did not stop.

What did a man say to a woman like that? Suppose now, just suppose he wanted to settle down . . . what would he say?

When night came he had not answered the question, and it was time to make camp. He reined his horse off the road, crossed over a low ridge and into an arroyo. His horse shied suddenly and when he looked ahead he saw the skeleton of a man. It was too dark to make out clearly, and the coyotes had been at it, but there it lay, and nearby were the bones of a horse, much of the hide still clinging to it. And there was the saddle.

He rode on a little farther, found a corner among the junipers and rocks, and settled down for the night.

The gent back there . . . that was how he'd die, most likely, and who would give a damn? When you rode alone you died alone, and there was nobody to do right by your bones.

"Well, mister," he said aloud, "I'll do right by you. Come daylight, I'll go back there and dig you out a grave. That's what I'll do."

Sleep came only after a long time of watching the stars. He saw the Big Dipper wheel around the sky, swore at his wakefulness, and finally fell to sleep. It was broad daylight when he awoke and the dun horse was nudging his toes.

He got up, dressed, and built a small fire. He boiled some coffee and fried a piece of venison, and when he had finished eating he got up, wiped his knife off on the seat of his pants, and shoved it back in the scabbard. It wasn't like Mrs. Teale's grub, but it was all right—it would do.

When he had saddled up he took his Winchester and walked back to the dead man.

By daylight the story was plain enough. The horse's leg was broken, snapped right off, and the position of the saddle and the crushed bones over the chest showed him all too clearly what had happened.

Somebody, an Indian most likely, had taken his rifle and pistol, if he'd owned them.

When Conagher had the grave dug he took hold of the skeleton and as he moved it he stirred some of the sand and revealed part of a coat still intact beneath the body. And partly under the edge of the coat and buried in the drift sand that had blown over it, were the dead man's saddlebags.

They were stiff and dry, the edges curled and turned kind of white, like the saddle itself. He pulled them apart when he couldn't get the stiff leather strap to come loose, and a shower of gold coins fell on the ground.

Startled, he stood for a moment looking down at them, then glanced around quickly.

But there was nobody—he was all alone.

He squatted on his heels and picked up the coins. He counted up to three hundred and twenty dollars, then shook out the saddlebags again. Five more gold eagles fell on the ground, and he picked them up.

Four hundred and twenty dollars—more than a year's wages, right there in his hands. And it was his —finders are keepers.

He looked through the remains of the saddlebags, but if there had been any letters or papers they had fallen apart and been blown away. He completed the burial, made a marker of a couple of big stones, and then mounted up.

Four hundred and twenty dollars! He was going into town and he was going to have himself a time. He was going to have one good blowout in his life, anyway—one at least.

He rode to Socorro and headed for a cantina.

The stage was standing on the street, and Charlie

McCloud was boosting a trunk toward the top. He glanced around, saw Conagher, and said, "Hey, give me a hand here!"

Together they got the trunk to the top and lashed it in place. McCloud dusted his hands, looking at Conagher thoughtfully. "I heard you were stopping over at Mrs. Teale's. I kind of thought you two would get together."

Conagher stared at the ground, flushing. "Aw, Charlie, you know I ain't the kind to stand hitched. I'm a drifter."

"How long have you been telling yourself that? You're no more a drifter than I am. Look, Conn, if you're smart you'll find yourself a piece of ground and settle down. That there's a fine woman."

"She is that. But she wouldn't have the likes of me. What have I got to offer a woman?"

McCloud chuckled. "Don't ask me. Let her tell you. A woman can always find something in a man worth having. I think you're a no-account saloon brawler who'd rather fight than eat, and the only things I can say good about you is that you do your job, you're honest, and you never backed off from trouble."

"Yeah. You can put that on my marker when they bury me. *'He never backed off from trouble.'* That's just what'll kill me, one of these days."

"Speaking of that, have you seen Kris Mahler? He's carrying a chip on his shoulder over you."

"It's one-sided. I've got no fight with him."

"Wasn't he one of the Parnell crowd there for a while?"

"I wouldn't know, but that's all over now, and I left that fight behind me."

"What are you aiming to do now?" McCloud asked.

"Charlie, I'm going to get drunk. I'm going to get mean drunk and then sleepy drunk, and when I wake up I'm going to ride clean to Montana or Oregon or somewhere far off."

He crossed the street and entered the cantina.

"Pedro," he said, "give me a bottle and that table over there. I'm going to get drunk."

"But señor," Pedro protested, "you do not get drunk! I have never seen you get drunk!"

"Nevertheless, I think—"

The door behind him swung inward. Conagher turned slowly. It was Kris Mahler.

"I heard you were in town," Mahler said. "So I came over to see what an honest man does when he's away from home."

Conagher felt a sudden, vast impatience. He did not want to fight, but there were times when it could not be avoided. He suddenly knew that one of them was going to leave town or else they were going to fight; and then he knew that he, at least, was not going to leave. He was going to stay.

He stood with his back to the bar watching Mahler with an expression of disgust.

Mahler came on into the room and stopped, legs spread apart, staring at him. There were only two others in the cantina, Pedro and Charlie McCloud, who had come in through the side door.

"Mahler, I'm minding my own business. I'm not looking for trouble."

"What's the matter? You turned yellow?"

"No, I just want no trouble. You've got it stuck in your craw because you rode off and I didn't, so what does it matter? That was your business, so let it lay."

"Suppose I don't want to?"

Mahler was a big man, a broad, strong man, powerfully made and rugged. "Ever'where I go," he said, "I hear what a tough man Conn Conagher is. Well, I've never seen any of your graveyards."

Conagher deliberately turned his back on Mahler and, taking up his bottle, crossed to the table he had chosen. He pulled out a chair and straddled it. Then he filled a glass.

"Damn you, Conn!" Mahler shouted. *"Listen* to me!"

"When you make sense, I'll listen. Come and have a drink."

Mahler took two long strides and swept the bottle and glass from the table, knocking them into a corner.

"All right," Conagher said mildly, "if you don't want to drink, pull up a chair and I'll order some grub. Or we'll just talk. I'm not going anywhere."

"That man you shot up in the hills back of Teale's, that was Hi Jackson. He was my saddle partner."

Conagher lifted his eyes. His smile was gone and his eyes were bleak. "That man was a damn rustler and a thief, and he tried to shoot me in the back."

Mahler grabbed for his gun, and Conagher, whose foot was lifted against the under frame of the table, shot the table out with one smashing kick, knocking it into Mahler.

He got up then and unbelted his guns and put them on the bar in front of Pedro.

Kris Mahler had gone down hard, but now he was getting up and Conagher walked up to him and hit him with a work-hardened fist. The blow caught Mahler in the mouth and staggered him, but he came in swinging. Conagher caught one and went to his knees, started up and caught another, a straight left that stabbed him in the mouth, and a right cross on the chin. He staggered back and brought up hard against the bar. Mahler's mouth was bloody, but he was smiling.

"If you want to take a beating," he said, "you'll get it. Nobody ever whipped me with their fists yet, and nobody ever will."

He feinted, then crossed another right to the jaw.

There was a smoky taste in Conagher's mouth, and he knew a tooth had been broken. Mahler could punch, and not only that, but he knew how to fight with his fists.

He came at Conagher, feinting, rolling to let Conn's right go by, then smashing him with two wicked punches in the belly. Mahler half stepped back then, expecting Conagher to fall, but Conn merely weaved, threw a left and a right that missed, caught a stiff left in the mouth, and then suddenly he ducked his head and lunged in.

The sudden attack when everything was going his way startled Mahler. He tried to side-step and bumped into a table, and Conagher smashed into him, knocking the table over and Mahler with it.

Conagher dropped swiftly, his knee driving into Mahler's stomach; then Conagher started to rise and as Mahler did the same Conagher's knee smashed him under the chin, knocking him back to the floor.

Mahler rolled over and Conagher sprang free, and as Mahler came up, Conagher went into him, hooking short and hard with both hands to the head and body. Shaken, Mahler backed up and tried to get set, but Conagher plunged into him, whipping up a wicked right to the wind, hooking a left that missed at close quarters, but smashing Mahler with an elbow.

They fought toe to toe, coldly, furiously. Conagher lost all track of time. He caught smashing blows to the head and the body, but grimly he dug in, hanging in there like a bulldog, taking Mahler's best shots and smashing back with both hands.

He backed Mahler against the bar, took two driving blows going in, and then leaned his head against Mahler's shoulder and ripped at his belly with short, wicked punches.

Conagher could taste blood in his mouth, and he knew there was blood on his face. He was knocked down, and then again. He got up, and felt a hammer-like blow on the side of the face, but as he swung he caught Mahler's arm and threw him hard against the piano. There was a thunder of sound and Mahler braced himself, but when he threw the punch Conagher went under it and ripped both hands to the wind, then moved back and brought up a right uppercut that broke Mahler's nose and showered him with blood.

Kris moved away. He kicked a chair out of the way for room in which to box. He jabbed, and jabbed again. He feinted, hooked a right to the chin, then tried the left, but Conagher had been waiting for it. He knocked the punch aside and whipped a lifting left into the solar plexus. Mahler's knees buckled and he started to fall, and Conn hit him again with a right. Mahler fell and Conagher caught him by the collar and jerked him upright and hit him three times more before the bigger man could fall again. He went down then, and he lay still.

Conagher stood over him, weaving and bloody, his shirt torn to shreds.

At last Conagher turned away and fell against the bar.

"You can have that bottle," Pedro said. "I give you the bottle."

"Don't want it," he mumbled, through broken lips. "I don't need it."

He was thinking. He was putting things together. The hammering he had taken left a confusion of ideas in his mind that suddenly began to be less confused; they began to fall into place.

Four hundred and twenty dollars in gold . . . Jacob Teale riding to buy cows . . . Jacob Teale never came back . . . a skeleton about one day's ride east . . . a dried-up saddle and saddlebags . . . it had to be.

He had both hands resting on the edge of the bar

and drops of blood were welling from his nose, and there was blood in his mouth. He spat.

His head was buzzing from the punches he had taken. He reached for his gunbelt in a staggering daze and buckled it on. Somebody handed him his hat.

"Mr. Conagher?"

It couldn't be. Not here. Not in Socorro. He turned his battered face toward the glare from the door and there a woman stood, framed against the sunlight. He could not see her face. Only a dress, a right pretty dress when you thought of it.

"Mr. Conagher? I think you should come home."

He stared at her. *Home*? He had no home. He took a step toward her and his knees buckled, but she caught him under the arm.

"Mr. McCloud? Will you help me? I am afraid he's hurt."

"*Him?* You couldn't hurt him with an axe. There's too much mule in him."

Conagher drew himself up. "Why did you come here?" he asked, swaying a little on his feet. He held his bandana against his bloody lips.

She was a plain woman, some had said, but she was pretty now, Conagher was sure of it.

"I . . . we need you, Mr. Conagher. I . . . we all felt lost . . . I don't know what . . ."

"There's the Ladder Five," he said, "that's a good outfit. I mean with this money . . . it's yours rightly . . . with this money we can buy some stock from Tay. We can make a start."

Kris Mahler rolled over and got up, his face twisting with pain. Holding his side he watched them go out the door. "I hit him," he said, "I hit him with ever'thing I had, and he still came at me."

He staggered against the bar, staring at the still swinging doors.

Outside Conagher fumbled in his pocket. He pulled out a small handful of shabby notes. "You . . . you wrote these, didn't you? I remember out there that night you said something about the wind in the grass, and—"

"I was lonely. I had to talk . . . to write to somebody, and there was no one."

"There was. There was me."

Back at the saloon Mahler shook his head. "I hit him," he said again. "I hit him with ever'thing I had. What sort of man is he?"

"He's Conagher," McCloud said, "and that's enough."

ABOUT LOUIS L'AMOUR

"I think of myself in the oral tradition—as a troubadour, a village taleteller, the man in the shadows of the campfire. That's the way I'd like to be remembered—as a storyteller. A good storyteller."

It is doubtful that any author could be as at home in the world re-created in his novels as Louis Dearborn L'Amour. Not only could he physically fill the boots of the rugged characters he writes about, but he has literally "walked the land my characters walk." His personal experiences as well as his lifelong devotion to historical research, that have combined to give Mr. L'Amour the unique knowledge and understanding of the people, events, and challenge of the American frontier, have become the hallmarks of his popularity.

Of French-Irish descent, Mr. L'Amour can trace his own family in North America back to the early 1600s and follow their steady progression westward, "always on the frontier." As a boy growing up in Jamestown, North Dakota, he absorbed all he could about his family's frontier heritage, including the story of his great-grandfather who was scalped by Sioux warriors.

Spurred by an eager curiosity and desire to broaden his horizons, Mr. L'Amour left home at the age of fifteen and enjoyed a wide variety of jobs including seaman, lumberjack, elephant handler, skinner of dead cattle, assessment miner, and officer on tank destroyers during World War II. During his "yondering days" he also circled the world on a freighter, sailed a dhow on the Red Sea, was shipwrecked in the West Indies and stranded in the Mojave Desert. He has won fifty-one of fifty-nine fights as a professional boxer and worked as a journalist and lecturer. A voracious reader and collector of rare books, Mr. L'Amour's personal library of some 10,000 volumes covers a broad range of scholarly disciplines including many personal papers, maps, and diaries of the pioneers.

Mr. L'Amour "wanted to write almost from the time I could walk." After developing a widespread following for his many adventure stories written for the fiction magazines, Mr. L'Amour published his first full-length novel, *Hondo*, in 1953. Mr. L'Amour is now one of the four bestselling living novelists in the world. Every one of his more than 85 novels is constantly in print and every one has sold more than one million copies, giving him more million-copy bestsellers than any other living author. His books have been translated into more than a dozen languages, and more than thirty of his novels and stories have been made into feature films and television movies.

Among Mr. L'Amour's most popular books are *The Lonesome Gods, Comstock Lode, The Cherokee Trail, Flint, Son of a Wanted Man, The Shadow Riders, Silver Canyon, Bowdrie*, the 18 novels featuring his fictional Sackett family, and his historical novel of the 12th century, *The Walking Drum*.

The recipient of many great honors and awards, in 1983 Mr. L'Amour became the first novelist ever to be awarded a Special National Gold Medal by the United States Congress in honor of his life's work. In 1984 he was also awarded the Medal of Freedom by President Ronald Reagan.

Mr. L'Amour lives in Los Angeles with his wife, Kathy, and their two children, Beau and Angelique.